The Man Who Was Taller Than God

The Man Who Was Taller Than God

Harold Adams

Walker and Company
New York

First published in the United States of America in 1992 by
Walker Publishing Company, Inc.;
first paperback edition published in 1998.

Published simultaneously in Canada by Thomas Allen & Son
Canada, Limited, Markham, Ontario

Library of Congress Cataloging-in-Publication Data
Adams, Harold, 1923–
The man who was taller than God/Harold Adams.
p. cm.
ISBN 0-8027-1239-8
I. Title
PS3551.D367M39   1992
813'.54—dc20   92-13260
CIP
ISBN 8-8027-7554-3 (paperback)

Printed in the United States of America
2 4 6 8 10 9 7 5 3 1

To Ivy Fischer Stone
agent, friend, and fan of a dozen years

▽

Preface

For the benefit of copyeditors, rookie readers of the Wilcox saga, and at least one critic from the past, let me offer a few points regarding this series.

The stories are placed in South Dakota during the 1930s, beginning in the last years of Prohibition. They extend beyond its repeal and are dominated by The Drouth. To South Dakotans, these two phenomena were always capitalized and distinct, and nobody I knew ever used the word *drought*.

The double disaster of Prohibition and The Drouth dominated every aspect of life in those days, but miraculously, no people of my acquaintance suffered fatal consequences from either curse. Perhaps more surprising, people laughed a lot, had a great time at the Saturday and Wednesday night dances in small towns like Clark, and celebrated the Fourth of July and Christmas with joy (and illegal spirits). The more adventurous sports drove to the Spider Palace at Stony Point on Lake Kampeska for dancing and worse. Most of them went to church on Sunday no matter how scandalously they'd behaved on Saturday night.

Before the thirties, I am told, the Ku Klux Klan was active and nasty, but having no blacks to abuse in that territory, they had to concentrate on Catholics, who were a convenient minority.

By the thirties this sort of thing had faded away enough so I was unaware of it as a child.

Except for the activities of my uncle, Sidney Dicky, who is the inspiration for Carl Wilcox, Clark had little crime that I'm aware of. The only occupants of the city jail, which was in the City Hall immediately east of the Adams Hotel where I lived each summer, were occasional drunks who either fell asleep on the street or made themselves nuisances in public. So far as I recall, none of them stayed longer than overnight.

There were, however, rumors of crimes, even murders, which never were solved. Until I created Carl.

The names used in these books, in many cases, are taken from deceased relatives and tolerant friends. Most come from my head, and none of the descriptions in appearance or character depict actual relatives or friends, living, dead, or spiritual.

The Man Who Was Taller Than God

▽

1

THE TOWN'S NAME WAS Hope. Some said it was originally
Lost Hope, others, Last Hope, but around Corden we just
called it Hopeless.

Actually it'd turned out okay for me because I got a job
painting street signs for the whole place, and while the pay
wasn't royal it covered my hotel room at five bucks a week,
took care of meals, and left some over for beer on Saturday
night. My Model T served as a portable paint shop.

It was nearing the end of a peaceful late July day when I
was nailing up the Grover Street sign and saw this kid pedaling wildly down the hill from the west. I recognized him
as the one who'd stopped to watch me roll a cigarette the
day before. He'd said his name was McGillacuddy and everyone called him Mac. I learned that night in the hotel he
was also called Cuddly and fought kids once a month trying
to convince them he was Mac.

He wheeled up hard beside me and skidded the rear wheel
around as he slammed on the brake.

"There's a guy in the sandpit," he told me, breathing hard.

"Yeah?"

"He's all bloody—dead or near—"

"Anybody you know?"

"Maybe—"

"How close'd you get?"

There was a second's hesitation before he said, close enough.

"Okay, pedal down to City Hall and tell Ruppman about it. I'll trot up and see if I can help."

It wasn't far enough to bother cranking up the Model T so I hiked over the ridge and a ways north off County 5. The pit had been dug out of a hill and was like a giant bowl tipped a bit up on the west and low toward the east. It was deeper than most I've known, with steep sides held firm by a three-foot depth of yellow clay along the top edges.

The body was visible from the pit rim and I dropped over the three-foot cliff onto sloping sand and scrambled to the bottom, where there were still signs of the old rut road dug by trucks hauling out their loads.

Mac was right. There was lots of blood and no sign of life in the long, lean body sprawled facedown in the sand. Flies, the closest thing South Dakota gets to buzzards, hummed around the ruined head, and black ants dashed about their business, avoiding the man's outstretched hand. He was wearing a navy blue suit, white shirt, black socks, and shiny black oxfords. All his pockets had been pulled inside out.

I was still squatting by the body when a Model A appeared over the ridge, wheeled down the gravel road, and parked nearby. Ruppman, the town cop, shut off the engine, got out carefully, gave me a nod without taking his eyes off the victim, and sighed.

Ruppman was so husky he seemed short, but came close to six feet tall. He had a wide nose, close-set eyes, and a wide, thin-lipped mouth. His suit, like the dead man's, was navy blue, but not so pressed or expensive.

"I don't like this," he told me. "Don't like it at all."

"You wanna bury him and forget it?" I asked.

"That there's Felton Edwards," he said, ignoring me. "Left Hope fifteen years ago. What'n hell's he doing here like this?"

Several answers came to mind, none of which he'd appreciate, so I dug out my tobacco bag and started building a smoke.

Ruppman squatted, examined the shattered head, looked up and down the long expanse of dead man, and shuddered.

"I figure he was shot in front, turned over, and searched," he said.

I agreed, although he hadn't asked my opinion.

"Robbery. But how in the hell'd he come to be here? Where's his car?" He looked up at me. "You check around any?"

"Nope. Came straight when Mac told me. You made it in a hurry."

"I gotta get Doc Williams. He's the coroner. And call some people. Jesus sweet Christ, what a mess. What was Mac doing out here?"

"Sandpits are places kids go."

"Yeah, well, this kid goes everywhere. Trust him to find a mess like this. You mind emptying your pockets?"

The only thing that surprised me about that remark was it had taken him so long to get around to it. I pulled both my front pockets out after removing my jackknife from the right one and six cents from the left, dug my bandanna out of my right rear pocket, a thin wallet from the left, and handed him the works.

"I don't really figure you went through his stuff," he told me, "but I gotta check."

I said right and asked if he wanted to go through my tobacco sack. He said no, I could hardly have stashed the man's wallet in that.

He gave me back my stuff, which I redistributed, and frowned when Mac came pumping down the hill on his bike.

"Well, Mr. McGillacuddy," Ruppman said as Mac came to a skidding halt, "did you find Doc Williams?"

"Uh-huh," said Mac, staring at the corpse. "Is he dead?"

"I'm not a doctor but I suspect he might be, since he's not breathing and hasn't brushed away any flies. Were his pockets turned out when you first saw him?"

Mac nodded.

"Okay, pedal on home and keep shut about this, understand?"

Mac frowned and said, "He's real tall, ain't he?"

"He was."

"You think he might've been taller than God?"

"I never thought about it. Might've been. Now get on."

"I paced him off," said Mac. "Figure he must've been six and a half feet tall."

"That's pretty close. So you didn't just come running for help, you stopped and measured him, huh?"

"Well, yeah," confessed Mac. "I never saw anybody that long before."

"How many dead men you seen?"

"Just Grandpa. He wasn't long at all."

"This kid," Ruppman told me, "has got a one-track mind."

I suggested maybe he wanted to think of something besides death.

"Goodbye, Mac," said Ruppman. "Please?"

As the boy pedaled off I reminded Ruppman that he hadn't asked the boy to empty his pockets. He shook his head. "He had time to stash anything if he did it but I don't believe he did, and nobody'd fault me if I missed even if he did heist it. Or do you figure maybe he shot him too?"

I admitted that was unlikely.

A black Buick came over the ridge and parked behind Ruppman's Ford. The driver climbed out with care, adjusted his suitcoat, and approached looking like a banker on his way to church.

Ruppman introduced him as Doc Williams. Doc gave me a nod and the corpse a look of cold disapproval.

"Recognize him?" asked Ruppman.

Doc looked doubtful, took a folded handkerchief from his pocket, placed it carefully on the sand, and went down on one knee to examine the head closely. He glanced at Ruppman.

"Felton, right?"

"Who else. See the height, the duds, and the crooked pinkie on his left hand?"

"Ah," said Doc respectfully, "you don't miss a thing, do you?"

"I don't know about that," said Ruppman as the doctor began examining the body. "Seems to me I've missed a lot. Don't ever remember being rich."

I laughed and drew a disapproving glance from the doctor.

"This is Carl Wilcox," Ruppman told him. "The fella from Corden doing our street signs."

"I've heard of him," said Doc Williams, and from the tone I guessed what he'd heard had nothing to do with my sign-painting talents.

"Yeah, well, don't believe it all, Doc. He's not old enough to've done half the things he gets credit or blame for."

Doc rose to his feet with so much grunting and effort he forgot to pick up his handkerchief and stared down at it a second trying to decide if it was worth stooping for. Ruppman saved him the trouble and Doc thanked him without sounding like he meant it.

"Did you tell Mac to have Joe come pick this up?" Ruppman asked him.

"I did. He's a very eager young'un."

Doc climbed back into his Buick and left. Ruppman started prowling around the body and asked me to see if there were any cars parked nearabouts. I circled the pit without seeing a car, truck, or bike. Ruppman came up to meet me in his Model A as I started back down the road and offered me a lift back to my car. On the way I asked him where Mac lived.

"Why?"

"Just curious."

"You did some police work in Corden, didn't you?"

I confessed to that.

"You don't need to do any here."

I said okay.

He gave me a squint, closed his car door, nodded, and drove off.

I put my tools back in my kit, placed it in the box on the right fender of the Model T, and drove back to the Cole Hotel.

Old man Cole looked up at the wall clock, then at his pocket watch, and said it must be nice for a man who could work his own hours. I said it was near as good as not working any, like him. That got me his lippy grin and a giggle.

"Hear you and Mac found Felton dead in the sandpit with his face all blowed in."

"It wasn't quite that messy," I said. "Did you know the guy?"

"Did once. Tallest man in South Dakota, I bet. And the craziest."

"What'd he do for a living?"

"Lotsa stuff. Ran the dance hall, had a general store for a while, sold farm machinery and insurance. Restless. Always up to something new. When he was real young he worked at the depot."

I sat in a rocker and rolled a smoke while he checked in a traveling salesman and told him all about Hope's murder. I was grateful he didn't point me out as the fella who'd found the body but realized quick he wasn't interested in sharing his tale.

When we were alone I asked him if he knew Mac McGilla-cuddy's parents. That got me a leering grin.

"Nobody knows that," he said.

"Who's he live with?"

"Schoolteacher named Florence Fogel. Some figure she's his natural ma. She says she's his aunt."

"Why you figure not?"

"Well, ten years back she was real thick with Johnnie Powers, the district judge's son. And when Johnnie went off to college in Minneapolis, all of a sudden she went too and two years later she was back with this one-year-old she said was her sister's boy. The sister, she claims, died in Iowa. What'd you think?"

I'd think it was none of my business but just shrugged.

"Besides," he said, "the kid's a dead ringer for Johnnie."

"Where do Mac and his aunt live?"

"Little bungalow on South Third. One set way back on the lot. Got two pines out front." He grinned. "She's a twenty-eight-year-old old maid."

I decided I ought to meet her.

$\triangledown$

2

Mac was hunched over his bike, oiling the New Departure brake, when I came up the front walk. I said it looked like he took good care of it.

He nodded as though that were too obvious for discussion and asked, was I here to see his aunt?

"Why'd I want to see her?"

"All the guys that come around do."

"There lots of them?"

"Some."

"As a matter of fact, you're the bird I was looking for. When I asked if the guy in the pit was somebody you knew, you said maybe. Why'd you say that?"

He screwed the cap back on his oil can and pushed it into the little bag hanging under the bicycle seat.

"He looked sort of familiar."

"Ruppman says he hadn't been around for fifteen years. Isn't that before your time?"

He looked me straight in the eye. "I guess I made a mistake. I was kind of excited."

"Okay. I just wondered. A guy that tall could hardly wander around Hope without somebody noticing, right?"

"Right. My aunt's around back. Weeding the garden."

"Flower or vegetable?"

"She's got both."

"Let's go look."

We walked around the small white house on crisp grass full of dandelions and found a trim woman seated on the back step drinking tea from a flowered cup. Her green-and-white dress looked old, which matched her brown shoes. Her hair was covered with a wide-brimmed straw hat and when she tilted her head to look at us I met hazel eyes that regarded me with something close to resignation, the kind of look mothers get when small boys bring home scruffy pets. Her nose was small and slightly tilted.

"This's Carl," Mac told her. "The sign painter."

"You should call him Mr. Wilcox, dear. How do you do? I'm Florence Fogel. I don't need any signs."

"I didn't expect you would. That's quite a garden. Must be a lot of work."

She looked at it with some satisfaction.

"In the summer I have a good deal of time for it. The trick is getting things planted early enough in spring to grow in our short season. In May I'm still busy at the school so I work rather desperately on weekends when the weather allows."

"It shows."

She smiled. I saw fine teeth, small dimples, and maybe something more.

"Is your visit here related to the man Mac found in the sandpit today?"

I said yes and told her what my question had been. She looked at Mac, whose attention stayed on me.

"Well," she said, getting up, "could I offer you a cup of tea?"

I said sure and she carried her cup into the house, saying she'd be right back. I walked over to the gardens. The vegetables were on the right, the flowers left. I recognized daisies, phlox, and tiger lilies, but couldn't name half a dozen others in bloom. The vegetables included about anything used in a salad.

She called Mac to open the door for her and brought out

a teapot, two cups with saucers, sugar and cream on a tray, set the whole business on the stoop, and, after sitting on the second step, poured for us. I accepted sugar and stirred before drinking. It was hot and strong.

"My grandmother," I told her, "could've made tea for two years with what you put in one pot."

"Is it too strong?"

"Nope, this is my style."

"I suspect," she said with a sly grin, "that you really prefer beer or something stronger."

"Not in tea."

She laughed and told Mac to go get cookies from the jar in the kitchen. He brought back a plate of date-filled ones, handed it to me, and went back inside.

"I understand you're a traveler," she said. "Where did you like it best of all you tried?"

"I usually like it best where I am."

"Then why roam so often?"

"So I won't get tired of it."

She laughed again and it almost closed her eyes. I liked the wide mouth, the smooth pale skin, and the blond hair that showed now she'd removed the hat.

"How come you didn't stay in Minneapolis?" I asked.

She sobered, sipped tea, and set the cup down. I expected she'd accuse me of snooping, but instead she seemed thoughtful.

"You know, I've often wondered. Ostensibly it was because I was offered a teaching job. Actually that was a rationalization. I wanted to be back in familiar surroundings with people I'd been comfortable with. It had nothing to do with returning to the old homestead, since I was born in North Dakota and moved here as a girl. I made friends in Hope High, or thought I had, and in Minneapolis all the students I was close to went away at term's end."

Her father, she said, had been a Lutheran minister and he and her mother had gone on a mission to Africa where they both died of dysentery.

"I never," she confessed, "understood why they left me with grandparents and went off that way. I guess they thought it'd be easier to make Christians of heathens there, but they certainly lost one here."

She glanced guiltily over her shoulder and laughed.

"I shouldn't talk like this. I never say such things to people in Hope, but from what I've heard, I guess you'd understand. You do, don't you?"

I tasted my third cookie and nodded.

She closed up after that. She felt she'd admitted too much. When I'd emptied my cup she offered no more but instead gathered up the tea things and asked me to hold the door when she carried them in. I thanked her and, after a good-bye to Mac, walked back to Main Street and drifted into a pool hall.

There was some ribbing from guys I'd played with the night before, and a stranger to me suggested a game of rotation. I could tell he was the local ace by the attitude of the onlookers, and from the first break it was plain this boy'd used a cue before. He had a fine touch but his luck wasn't too great, so I had to go gently for him to win. Everybody felt real good about it and I only lost two bucks. Of course he wanted more and I let him talk me into it. His luck improved and he won the second round pretty much on his own. He offered me a chance to get even by doubling the stakes and I agreed. When I won he wanted to go another round and I said thanks, but he was too tough to fight all night and I'd quit while I was even.

He got snottier about that than seemed polite and finally I told him if he was that excited about it I'd be glad to settle the matter outside. He decided against it.

In bed that night I figured it hadn't been too bad a day.

3

THUNDER WOKE ME FRIDAY and then rain slapped the windows and drizzled down, distorting all outside. I watched some smart flashes and listened to the crack of close strikes followed by a ripping that sounded as if the sky was tearing apart, and finally it came down to a mean rumble. The hotel croaked and groaned in the howling wind.

I pulled on pants and shoes and made a swing around to the toilet but somebody had beat me to it. I heard it flush and waited. A moment later a tousled redhead came out, gave a start at the sight of me, and turned her head to hide. It embarrassed her sick I'd heard the flushing.

"Some thunder," I said, trying to be reassuring, but that only made her tuck her chin lower and move faster. She probably thought I'd heard her fart. Somehow proper ladies seem to have the most active imaginations when it comes to making nasties out of innocent remarks.

The seat was still warm when I parked on it and I grinned, thinking the redhead would probably imagine I'd discover that and consider it another humiliating intimacy.

Back in my room I napped awhile despite the storm, knowing there'd be no place I could get coffee, let alone breakfast, before light. Besides, until the rain quit and things dried I couldn't get any work done, so I might as well loaf.

It was near nine-thirty when I hiked the half block west to Winkle's Café. I sat at the counter and ordered pancakes, bacon, and coffee from Mary, the chubby, short-haired waitress.

"You're late," she told me.

"No, the rain was early."

She snickered. Almost anything you said produced that.

"I suppose," I said, "you're too young to remember rain in South Dakota?"

"Go on, seen it twice. Is that gonna be enough syrup?" she asked, nodding at the nearby pitcher.

"If it isn't you can just smile on the stack."

That brought another snicker and then she moved off. I saw movement out of the corner of my eye and turned to spot the bathroom redhead coming in the front door. She sailed directly to a booth across the café from me, slipped in, and concentrated on the menu she found tucked between the sugar bowl and syrup pitcher.

Her hair was neatly brushed now but mostly covered by a black hat she hadn't bought anyplace in South Dakota. Her raincoat, which she slipped off after sitting down, was light tan.

Mary went over and took her order. It called for lots of consultation. The contrast between them was something—Mary's pug nose, round cheeks, double chin, and mousy hair against a straight, narrow nose, bony cheeks, a sharp chin, and flaming hair.

"Pipe that," Mary muttered out of the corner of her mouth as she passed behind me, "Lady bloody Astor."

"Very tony," I allowed. "Know her?"

She shook her head and went into the kitchen. I saw Ed Winkle, the café owner and cook, come to the swinging doors and peer through the small square of glass at his customer. You could use a picture of Ed's face for a model of any cheerful jack-o'-lantern you'd care to carve.

The rain kept up and I stayed at the counter, drinking

coffee and smoking after I'd finished breakfast. The redhead got scrambled eggs, toast, and jelly and drank milk. She left without glancing any direction but the one she was heading in.

Mary came over and leaned on the counter before me.

"No, I don't know who she is and don't care. She's the type that orders without looking at you. I hate that kind."

"She's staying at the hotel."

"Really? You saw her there?"

"Oh yeah. We're sharing different rooms together."

She looked shocked, then grinned and finally laughed, telling me I was a caution.

It was still raining when I went out. I was wearing a slicker I'd owned since cowboy days and a slouch hat that made me look like the villain in a Western. The combination kept me dry down to my shoes and there were few puddles on the sidewalk, so for a while I moved in comfort. The wind that brought the storm had died down.

I passed the bakery and the sweet smell was enough to revive the appetite I'd killed with pancakes. Then there was the soda fountain, with soda glasses painted on the windows by some guy who should never have handled anything but a manure fork. The meat market was next and then a hardware store and beyond that a jeweler's. I didn't see any customers in any of them and wondered what the hell the proprietors did besides stare out their windows when nobody came in. Bakers could bake and butchers carved carcasses, but what could a jeweler or a soda man do to pass his time?

I went into the combination newsstand, tobacco shop, and pool and beer hall and gawked at the few slick magazines and bunches of pulps including Spicy Detective, Western, and Romance.

Sex was more dear, the Spicy's were a quarter apiece. Regular pulps went for a dime, and so did the slicks, except *Liberty*, which was a nickel.

I popped for a *Black Mask* (a dime), carried it back to the hotel, and was stopped by old man Cole's sly grin in the lobby.

"I guess you went around to meet Mac McGillacuddy's aunt," he said.

"How'd you figure that?"

"Officer Ruppman was around to see you right after you went for breakfast."

"Couldn't he figure out where I'd be?"

His grin broadened. "I guess you don't know. He's sweet on Miz Fogel. Probably wants to talk with you more private than at Winkle's."

The rain was slacking off as I headed for City Hall, where Cole said I'd find the town cop.

Ruppman was sitting beside a table in a small room on the left side of a short hall. A bare bulb hung over him, casting stingy light over the floor.

"Cole says you were looking for me."

He nodded, took his feet off the chair in front of him, and shoved one leg so it turned my way.

"Sit down."

I took off my hat and parked.

"I went over to see Mac," I said.

He nodded. "Why?"

"When he first talked to me after finding the body, he said he thought the man was somebody he'd seen. That was interesting, since you say the man's been gone the last fifteen years."

"He hadn't lived here in fifteen. No reason he couldn't stop by. So what'd Mac say?"

"He said he probably made a mistake."

He stared at me, shifted impatiently, and said okay, so then I'd talked with the aunt. There was a break before he said "aunt," and I sensed he knew I caught that.

"Yeah. Mac suggested I talk with her. I think he wanted to switch attention from himself."

"Did it work?"

I smiled. "Pretty good. I didn't want to try rubber-hosing him for a straight answer and thought maybe something'd develop. When I mentioned the question to his aunt she gave him a look but didn't push and after that he just faded out of the picture."

"You mean you didn't notice him any more?"

"I mean he left us alone."

Ruppman nodded, swiveled his chair a couple inches, and rested one elbow on the table beside him.

"Mac's a smart kid, wouldn't you say?"

I agreed.

"You're not too slow yourself, are you?"

I tried a modest smile.

"It seems to me I mentioned to you yesterday I didn't need any help doing police work. I'm mentioning it again. You just stick with your sign painting, understand?"

"How far does police work spread?"

"Some past Florence."

"That's what I figured."

$\triangledown$

4

THE RAIN HAD STOPPED and high winds were herding clouds away when I got back outside. In Hope, like Corden, rain or shine, weekdays and Sunday you could walk the length of the main drag without seeing a soul astir on the sidewalks or a car pass on the street. So naturally I piped the high-toned redhead when she was a block west walking my way from the hotel. If she noticed me she kept it a secret, and a quarter of a block away halted, stared at an entryway on her left, checked the number, and went in. I strolled over and backed up a couple steps to take in the windows on the second floor. The one on the right was lettered in black, ERIC ATWATER, ATTORNEY AT LAW. The other, in identical lettering (which needed retouching), read DR. EDWARD THORPE, DENTIST.

I wondered why it wasn't "Dentist at Health" or something like and then considered whether an attorney could be anything but "at law."

In either case I figured the redhead was in trouble and couldn't decide which was worse. Probably the lawyer, since the pain they inflict usually lasts well beyond the time you sit before them.

I ambled a couple blocks west to the edge of town and stared off across the prairie. It was hard to remember when corn and wheat billowed green in the wind as far as you could see. Now it was sunburned crisp where the ground wasn't bare. The wind was up again and had already dried the earth and was whipping dust north. Off to my right railroad tracks flanked by telephone poles and wires merged toward the horizon, reminding me of my days in empty boxcars with no responsibilities like an aging Model T and signs to paint. Nothing to worry about except where my next meal was coming from, how to duck the railroad bulls, and what would cure body lice.

Somehow I didn't miss any of that a damned bit.

I started back toward the main drag and considered the sign-painting job, but it was so near noon it seemed practical to postpone it till after lunch.

I was passing the newsstand etc. when Christian Frykman, the town mayor, who'd hired me to paint the signs, came out behind me and called my name. I halted and turned to meet him.

He was tall and gaunt, with a shock of mixed blond and white hair he'd never been able to tame with a brush. The strong jaw and bony cheeks gave his face a fierce Viking shape, but his eyes were sad.

"Got a minute?" he asked. His voice matched the eyes. It seemed meant for delivering funeral sermons.

"I think I can spare one."

He nodded soberly and suggested we cross the street to Winkle's for a cup of coffee. Mary greeted him warmly and followed us over to the booth he picked. It was where the redhead had eaten breakfast.

"The signs look good," he told me when Mary had taken our orders for coffee and left. "Very satisfactory."

I thanked him.

"You know of our tragedy," he said. "I understand you were one of the first to see the body."

I nodded.

"There's never been a murder in Hope before," he said. "At least not since the city was formally established. I believe there was some sort of unfortunate death in a family in the late 1880s, before the charter, but it was never determined whether that was accidental or otherwise."

He wasn't fishing for reactions at this point so I didn't offer any, just gave him the attention he was used to. Suddenly he smiled gently and shook his head.

"I'm uncertain of the best way to get at this," he said apologetically. "Forgive me if I ramble like an old man."

"You're doing fine."

"Well, have you heard anything about Felton, the victim?"

"I know he was tall."

"Yes, I think perhaps that was a curse for him. He seemed to feel he had to do more than other men, be more assertive and successful. He wasn't really clever enough to succeed. Or perhaps I should say wise. But then, foolish men do often succeed, don't they?"

"You want me to find out who killed him?"

He sighed gratefully and hunched over the table. "Would you?"

"Ruppman seems like a good man," I said. "He knows the town and people better than I do."

"Sometimes that can be a handicap. Emotional involvement is a poor support for judgment and Officer Ruppman, on occasion, is rather impulsive."

"You think Florence Fogel's connected with the murder?"

His eyes narrowed. "You're aware of his interest in her?"

"He sort of brought it to my attention."

"Ah." He shook his head sorrowfully. "That's part of what I meant. But no, I don't wish to imply that Florence had anything to do with it. Although she did know Felton. I'm afraid every attractive woman in Hope or anywhere else, knew Felton. Florence has always been a girl men noticed. Very pretty, vivacious—"

"I thought Johnnie Powers was her big moment."

"Johnnie was deeply involved with Florence back when

she was eighteen or so. I guess you've been talking with Cole. He's our foremost gossip."

"Does he get things straight?"

"Occasionally. A man who talks as much as he does is bound to strike truth now and then."

"Is it true Florence went with Powers to Minneapolis?"

"Not exactly. He went first, she went after."

"And came home with a year-old kid."

"Her nephew. Yes. There was some problem with that among members of the school board but it was finally settled in her favor."

"You mean they didn't think she'd ought to be hired?"

"That's right."

"You on the school board?"

"Yes."

I guessed he was the chairman but didn't press it.

He began telling me about Felton Edwards. He said as a boy he'd been an erratic student, getting high marks in math and barely passing English, and frequently caused discipline problems. He wasn't interested in sports, had a doting mother, and a father who often referred to him as a freak. By the time he was in high school boys learned it was wise to leave him alone. He was exceptionally strong despite his slenderness, and quick-tempered. No one made fun of his height more than once.

He sipped the coffee Mary had delivered and looked sad.

"You said all the attractive women attracted Felton—did that include married ones?"

"Oh yes. The state of matrimony was never a deterrent to Felton, his or anyone else's. His wife had diabetes, went blind, and finally died of it. A very sweet girl but pretty much of an invalid her last years. It was a hard time for Felton."

It didn't sound too sweet for his wife.

"So whose wives did he get cozy with?"

He squirmed some but when I told him I couldn't get anything done without all the background, he sighed and went on.

"He was friendly with Kay Bostrom, Ted's wife at the grocery store, and Lucy Friar, Buster's wife. He runs the jewelry store. Far as I know neither one of them's ever owned a gun and they're not vindictive men. I feel confident that whoever shot Felton was someone from his life outside of Hope."

I decided Mayor Frykman wasn't exactly objective about his town's citizens.

"So what do you want from me?" I asked.

"Well, we have no town funds to hire an investigator, but I can pretty much guarantee you a good many painting jobs if you're able to help on this little problem. You know anyone in Edenberg?"

I said I thought there were a couple Corden characters who'd moved there that I could contact. Edenberg was about five times the size of Corden and guys with modest ambitions chose it over the greater risk of Minneapolis.

"Fine," said Frykman. "You can make some telephone calls from my house. I'll pay. Let's see if we can get a lead on what Felton's been up to since he left Hope."

"Ruppman won't like me messing into this."

"You leave Officer Ruppman to me. What we'll do is, you'll have dinner at my house tonight. My housekeeper's a better than fair cook. You'll eat well."

That hit me in my next-to-weakest spot. I said okay.

$\triangledown$

5

MAYOR FRYKMAN'S HOUSE WAS surrounded by half the trees in Hope and stood on the highest rise in town. When I knocked at the front door after crossing half a block of open porch, a gangling woman opened up and looked me over as if she'd just found something wriggly under a rock.

"I'm Carl Wilcox," I said.

"You look it," she told me, and with reluctance stepped back to let me in.

From the amount of furniture and gewgaws it seemed more like a market than a home. The walls were covered with dark paper, heavy drapes kept out daylight, and cluttery chandeliers couldn't whip the shadowiness even with all the bulbs burning. It was a place that called for candles, but they'd have needed a lackey working full-time to keep them lit and snuffed each day.

Laverne (I learned her name later from Frykman—she didn't bother to offer it herself) led me to the master's study, and he looked up from a rolltop desk big enough for conversion to a bungalow. For a second his face was blank, as if I'd been forgotten. Then he tilted back in his judge's chair and nodded me toward an overstuffed one in the corner.

"I hope you brought a healthy appetite."

I didn't tell him tramps are always hungry.

He had already called the Edenberg telephone operator and got numbers for three people I'd named before we parted earlier.

"It'll be better to call after supper," he said. "How's the job going?"

"Fine."

"I talked with Ed Winkle and Ted Bostrom and both'd like you to do window signs for them when you're through with the street signs. That should lead to other jobs. Ed wants to pay off in meals—is that all right?"

I nodded.

He considered me for a few moments. Finally he said, "I understand you play pool."

I confessed that was true.

"Larson tells me he thinks you may have made a living at it."

I guessed Larson was the poolroom owner.

"If I was that good, I wouldn't paint signs."

"He suggests that's a front. He admits you haven't won a great deal yet, but he worries."

"Maybe he's in the wrong business."

He thought about that a moment, glanced at papers on his desk, and looked at me again.

"I'd appreciate it if you'd avoid trouble while you're working for me. The pool hall doesn't attract our better element and it'd be very awkward if folks thought you skinned some of our boys. It'd be even worse if that sort of thing led to a brawl. I'm aware you can take care of yourself, but you could embarrass me."

I twitched a little and managed a smile. "I don't know, Mr. Mayor. I'm beginning to feel hedged in. Ruppman warns me off Florence and you tell me don't play pool. Is it okay if I drink a beer?"

"Carl, I don't care what you do as long as you don't embarrass me. And you've got to admit, your past is enough to give me concern."

Laverne called us to dinner and we were too busy with fine juicy pork chops, boiled potatoes with great brown gravy, and sweet corn on the cob to consider potential embarrassments for quite a while. After that we ate fresh apple pie.

Later, in the living room, he stoked a pipe while I rolled a cigarette and we both smoked. He asked about murders in Corden connected with the football anniversary party the fall before and I told him how it all worked out.

Then I made the telephone calls.

The first guy had moved to California and the lady who answered seemed glad of it. The second said he remembered Felton Edwards, but only because he was the tallest man in town. He thought maybe he'd been involved in running a dance hall weekends and was fairly sure he sold insurance.

The last resource was Dick McCoy. He was branch manager for a national insurance outfit and a big man with the local American Legion. It took a while for him to remember me, and then all he wanted to talk about was when they'd hired me to put on a rope-twirling show that climaxed with my lassoing the Legion's drum major.

His chatter came to a whoa when I butted in and told him I was checking on Felton Edward's murder. He didn't ask how come I was, so I figured he'd heard something of my recent doings.

Finally he said Felton had worked as an insurance salesman for him about a dozen years or more. He'd been an uneven producer, going great guns for up to three months, then loafing four or five. McCoy admitted, reluctantly, that in general customers liked him. He was a good storyteller and colorful enough that folks got a kick out of swapping stories about his height, crazy lies, and woman-chasing.

"He first came to Edenberg peddling cash registers for some national outfit but they dumped him in the second year. Too unreliable. I think there was some woman problem somewhere."

"He ever remarry?"

"Hell no. Not after his first experience. Had a couple

steadies, I hear. One a fresh widow and the other still attached to a husband."

The widow's name was Agatha Hendrickson; the married one was Pauline Clint. Polly. Her cuckold was Leslie. McCoy said Leslie was the biggest undertaker in town, real loaded, busier than ants in a cookie jar, and dumb enough to think Felton was a funny, harmless guy with a big appetite for his wife's cooking.

"About six months ago Felton quit me. Said there was no damned future in insurance and just disappeared."

I asked about jealous husbands and boyfriends and he allowed there were a lot of both, but none he knew of had ever threatened murder or seemed capable of it.

Frykman listened to my account of McCoy's ramblings after I hung up and sat scowling thoughtfully for some time. Then he nodded his head.

"The first thing for you to do," he said, "is drive to Edenberg and spend the weekend. Talk to those two women the man says Felton was involved with. Find out what happened to make him suddenly leave town."

My face must've told him I wasn't tickled with the assignment, but he assured me right away he'd cover all my expenses and find a way to pay a bonus if my investigations bore fruit.

"Just keep a smart record," he told me. "I've talked with Joey, the officer in Corden. He assures me you're basically honest and persistent once you're on a trail, and that's all I'm asking for."

So what the hell. I enjoy hotels where I don't have to help run them. Saturday morning I left Hope and headed for Edenberg.

6

It was near noon when I walked into McCoy's office downtown. His face was a study when he looked up from his desk by the front window and piped me. In his world acceptable types never had broken noses or went without a tie. I guessed he suddenly wished he had a private office in the back. He managed to dredge up a smile, got to his feet, and offered his soft hand while trying to figure out how he'd explain this bum to his hired help or any customers who might happen by and gawk in. The receptionist by the door smiled tolerantly when I glanced her way as I trailed McCoy back to his desk. I wondered if she knew her boss had been born in Corden but guessed, knowing him, he claimed to have come from Minneapolis or maybe someplace even farther east.

He asked about my folks. I said they were tolerable. He wanted to know if Bertha still ran the kitchen and I said yes. After all the preliminaries he gave me a map of Edenberg and pointed out where the ladies in question lived.

When I tried to pump him for more names of people who'd known Felton he looked at his watch, apologized, and said he had to leave for a luncheon engagement. I let him crowd me out of the office and accepted his handshake before he got into his Oldsmobile parked out front, waved cheerfully, and drove off.

When he turned the first corner I about-faced and went back to see the receptionist.

She was, as Ma would say, approaching middle age. Her dark brown hair was flecked with gray, there were experience lines around her large eyes, and laugh wrinkles framed her mouth. A little sign on her desk read MRS. SIMPSON.

I asked if she'd been with McCoy long and she said yes, over a dozen years.

"So you knew Felton?"

"Oh yes, indeed."

"I heard he was quite a fella."

She agreed with a warm smile.

"You know what happened to him?"

Her face went into mourning. "Mr. McCoy told me. It's awful."

I glanced at the wall clock and asked if I could take her to lunch. She blinked, blushed, and said, "Well, I—"

"If your husband wouldn't mind?"

"No, I lost him seven years ago—"

"I'd like to know what you know about Felton. It might be helpful."

"Oh, you mean, in finding out who—?"

I nodded soberly.

She opened the bottom drawer of her desk, got her purse, and stood erect. "I'd be only too happy to help."

Her first name was Lois and she was built for comfort, not for speed. We got a booth at a place half a block west of the office where everybody knew her and tried to keep an eye on us without being too obvious. She enjoyed the stir.

"People'll be talking about this for a month," she told me, "but I don't care. Whoever killed Felton shouldn't be allowed to get away with it."

We both had the hot pork sandwich, which came steaming and tasted grand. She let me know that folks exaggerated Felton's weakness for the ladies.

"Oh sure, he was a flirt, but there was no harm in him. He flirted with everyone, even me, but there was nothing to it but just natural friendliness. I think most of the talk came from people who were jealous of his height and abilities."

"Why'd he leave the insurance business?"

"Oh, he said he was bored with it and I suppose that was true. He did get bored easily and he was very ambitious. Felton could sell shoes to mermaids if he wanted but he was a dreamer and always wanted to do something more grand."

"You don't know where he went from here?"

She shook her head.

"Didn't he get mail after he left? Where'd you forward stuff?"

"General delivery in Aquatown."

I asked who his Edenberg friends were but she couldn't name any. She said other salesmen with the company were put off by his casual success. They resented him being able to outsell them working only half as hard and, she admitted ruefully, he was inclined to rub it in.

"He told Tommy Bingston, right here in the office, that he had to take it easy or all the other salesmen'd be out of work."

She asked me about my involvement and I said I'd been hired, by people I couldn't name, to investigate the murder.

"You could tell me who," she said. "I never gossip."

I smiled mysteriously.

"Well," she smiled, "where're you from?"

"Corden. I was a cop there a little while back. Lately I've been doing some work in Hope and happened to be the first grown-up to see the body. It was found by a kid who came and told me."

She wanted to know what kind of work I'd been doing in Hope and I gave her another mysterious smile, which made her eyes glow. She just loved mysteries—and I liked her smile, and didn't mind her being older than me.

"You got a boyfriend?" I asked.

She blushed. "No, I'm too old for that."

"Really? You don't look anywhere near eighty. How'd you like to take in a movie with me tonight?"

I wasn't sure Frykman would agree this was a business expense he'd cover but figured it was worth a try.

"Oh no, I couldn't—"

"What's the matter, you think your boss'd be sore?"

That flustered her even more than my offer, and I wondered if there might be something between them. She denied that she'd thought of Mr. McCoy being offended, but finally admitted he might be, since he was very strong on appearances.

"He's a phony, isn't he?"

She drew back. "I thought you were his friend!"

"He's an acquaintance, Lois. He hired me once and that was it. You're not old enough to bury yourself, and what you do on your own time is your business, right?"

"A woman who works full-time in this town has no time or business that's private," she told me sternly. "Not unless she owns the business, and I don't know any who do."

I couldn't recover ground after that, and when we left the café she said she knew her way back, thanks for the lunch, and good-bye.

It took me maybe a second to shake off all the scorn she'd laid on and then I looked up Agatha Hendrickson's number in a hotel telephone booth, gave her a call, and heard a low, almost husky hello.

She listened to my name and a quick story about being an investigator looking into Felton Edwards's death. Would she have time to see me?

There was a moment of no sound but the line's hum. Then she asked who I was working for. I told her I couldn't say. The wire hummed some more.

"You know my address?"

I did. She said to come, and hung up.

It was a white clapboard duplex, with gray trim and an enclosed front porch. I passed through the unlocked outer door and saw two inner doors side by side, with names over each of the bell presses. Hendrickson was on the right, upstairs. I poked the button and a moment later saw movement through the curtained glass door, just before the knob turned and a woman pulled it open and stared at me. She was easily twenty years younger than McCoy's receptionist and at first glance I didn't think she'd ever develop laugh wrinkles. Her wide mouth dipped at the corners, and a frown furrowed what I guessed could be a brow smooth as ivory in her better moments.

I apologized for bothering her and asked when she'd heard of Felton's death.

"This morning. On the radio. Come in. My nosy neighbor's breaking her neck to see you."

She stepped aside and waved me up the stairs. Evidently she'd read the same etiquette book as Ma, which said ladies always precede men downstairs but follow them up.

I stopped in the small hallway at the head of the steps and let her lead me into a cream-walled living room with a fireplace opposite the door, flanked by white bookshelves filled with fat and thin volumes, a good many of them leatherbound. She noticed where I looked and asked if I were a reader.

I confessed I'd hit a book or two in my time.

"Who do you like?"

"Will James, Twain, Doyle, Zane Gray—"

"Who's Will James?"

"A cowboy. Wrote about horses and the West."

"How about Cooper?"

"Not much."

She proved she could smile. It didn't light up the room but it raised the temperature a notch. She waved me toward a couch on my left and sank into a dark chair near the bookshelves, to the right of the fireplace. I noticed her ankles were slim. She knew I noticed.

"You look like a cowboy."

"I was," I admitted. "I thought these pants were too loose to show my bowlegs."

The smile turned on again and I decided it did light up the room.

"What do you want from me?"

"I'm trying to get a lead on why Felton went to Hope Wednesday night and what he might've been carrying that made somebody search the body."

She flinched at the last word, and her gaze moved from me to the front windows in the sun porch, beyond an arch to my left. It was the first hint she'd given that the death meant anything to her.

After a moment she looked back at me.

"Would you like coffee?"

"Sure."

She smiled as she rose. "I like that. People who pussyfoot around saying 'If it's no bother' give me a pain."

She walked through the dining room and into the kitchen beyond. I realized she wasn't padded, as I'd assumed at first glance. Her hips were almost slim under the snug-fitting blue dress.

I went over to the bookshelves and saw the *Encyclopaedia Britannica* across the bottom row and above it a set of Hawthorne novels, Jane Austen, poetry by Shelley, Keats, and Byron, and *The Rubáiyát of Omar Khayyám*. I was looking at a fat book named *Look Homeward Angel* when she came back carrying two mugs of coffee with a cream and sugar set on a round tray.

"You read him?" she asked, nodding at the book in my hand.

I shook my head. "Looks pretty heavy."

"He's not like anyone else. Sort of ponderous poetic. I don't think a cowboy'd like it."

I didn't tell her I'd outgrown cowboying and put the book back on the shelf.

She went to the kitchen for a spoon when she saw me take sugar, came back, handed it to me, and sank into her big chair.

"I've no idea what Felton might've been doing in Hope.

He hated the place. We've been out of touch for over six months. I wish I could honestly tell you I told him to take a hike but it wasn't that way. He lost interest. I think he preferred his married woman because there'd be no chance of getting hooked into marriage, but maybe that's just sour grapes. Our relationship was impossible anyway. I can't understand why I didn't break it off myself. Felton was a very selfish man. And mean. I know I'm being awful to talk like this when he's been murdered, but I put up with so much it's a relief knowing it is absolutely over."

She shook her head sadly.

"This is incredible. I'm telling you things I've barely admitted to myself over the past year, and I never saw you before. I guess it's something that's just been building up for so long, and I never had anybody I could talk to about it . . ."

"You didn't happen over to Hope Wednesday night and blow him away, did you?"

For a second I thought she was going to get mad, but then she gave a nervous laugh and shook her head again.

"No. I wasn't that worked up. Nowhere near."

"I didn't think you would be."

"You might consider his lady friend's husband," she said very casually.

"You think he was jealous?"

"He certainly had reason to be. Although from what I hear, I guess he was a perfect patsy. But maybe they got careless and let him catch them together. I guess there's a limit to every man's tolerance."

"I doubt if he caught them in the Hope sandpit."

"With Felton, you never know. About anything could happen."

$\triangledown$

7

Before I left Agatha told me she taught fourth grade at the nearby elementary school and had met Felton after her father died. He'd been her father's insurance agent and came around to visit when the policy paid off.

"He pretended he just wanted to offer condolences and gab about what a great old man Dad had been, and I fell for it. Now I think he was looking for business or thinking of a way to get at the insurance money. That's probably the real reason he finally lost interest—he knew I was too close to let any of it go."

She was trying to laugh it off but I could tell none of it was funny to her.

When I made to go she asked if I was planning a visit with Pauline Clint. I said yes.

"Have you called her yet?"

I hadn't, so she suggested I use her phone.

Pauline's voice wasn't as sexy as Agatha's, but came on friendly until I explained what I wanted to see her about. Then it turned guarded.

"I understand," I said, innocent as a cherub, "that you and your husband were good friends of his, and I need to

learn all I can about the man to find out who killed him.
Would you rather I came around when your husband was at
home?"

She said it'd be best to come this afternoon. Now, if convenient.

Agatha smiled after I hung up and asked me to let her know
what I learned. "I'm dying to know what she'll say about me.
Why don't you come for dinner? I'll fix something here."

I agreed.

The Clint house was on a corner three blocks from downtown. I gaped at its size and the sign proclaiming it CLINT'S
FUNERAL HOME. The grounds and building filled at least
two, maybe three lots, with two fancy entrances, one facing west, the other south. It was tall, broad, clean, and
landscaped with a lawn that came the closest to carpet of
any I'd seen in South Dakota. I walked along the south
side and decided that was the business entrance, so I
moved around the corner and approached the residential
door. A blond woman appeared, observing me from behind
the screen.

"Mrs. Clint?" I asked.

"Mr. Wilcox," she replied. I was ushered in and followed
her down a broad hall into a sunken living room on the right.
It was a parlor grand enough to make Ma swoon. Persian
carpets, whopping portraits on the walls with frames fancy
enough for royalty, and furniture all fat and deep-cushioned
and draped with dinky scarves to protect places where hands
rest and heads touch. I felt maybe I should take off my shoes
before walking in, but brazened it out, plunked my two-bit
fanny on her two-hundred-dollar chair, and told her it was
a cozy room.

"Garish is more like it," she said with a flip of her jeweled
hand, and sat facing me on a rose-trimmed couch. "What
do you want to know?"

I thought it was interesting she didn't show any curiosity
about my poking into the whole affair.

"When'd you see Felton Edwards last?"

"I don't know, maybe six months ago. Time flies, doesn't it?"

"Did he tell you he was leaving town?"

"Not exactly. He said he had new prospects. I don't recall that he elaborated on that."

"Was he here for supper or . . . ?"

"It was lunch."

"You didn't ask about the prospects?"

"He was vague. I'll admit that by that time I'd become a little weary of his grand ideas about getting rich. He got a new inspiration about once a month."

"Like what?"

"Well, the latest was opening a tavern. He was going to get a job selling liquor—said he'd learn the business from the ground up, then get investors and build a place, maybe two or even three."

"He ask your husband to invest in this?"

She had oriental eyes, so slanty and narrowed they half hid the iris. Her brows were plucked into thin lines painted black, and the mascara on her lashes was thick enough to make them sag. She peered at me from under all that.

"No. I told Les it'd be money down the drain."

"Was that during your last lunch with Felton?"

She nodded.

"Did he get sore?"

She tipped her head against the chair back. "What does that question have to do with the murder?"

"I don't know. Did he get mad?"

"He didn't have a tantrum, if that's what you're getting at. I explained why I didn't think my husband's funeral business would mix well with taverns. He accepted that calmly and left."

"And you never heard from him again."

"That's right."

"I heard you and Felton were real close. You think he broke

off because you weren't willing to risk your husband's dough in a deal you didn't trust?"

"You've been listening to gossip. Felton was a common friend to me and my husband. That's all there was to it. I wasn't his mistress, whatever you're implying or may have heard."

"Do you know Agatha Hendrickson?"

"The name's vaguely familiar. She's a schoolmarm, isn't she?"

"Uh-huh. The one gossips say was your chief rival."

She brought her head away from the chair back.

"I take it you've talked with her already. Did you find her deep in mourning?"

"Not too deep."

"Well," she waved her sparkling hand again, "who knows? Perhaps Felton's death was at the hand of the lady scorned."

"She thought there was a good chance a jealous husband did it."

She smiled thoughtfully, like a cat burying its business.

"Perhaps so, but it certainly couldn't have been mine."

"Fine. Where'd I find him this afternoon?"

"In Minneapolis."

"Got a number where I can reach him?"

"No. He calls me. If I hear I'll tell him you want to talk with him."

"Fine. I wouldn't want to say anything wrong, so maybe I ought to know if he's heard the gossip about you and Felton."

"How thoughtful. Yes, he has. We've laughed about it often."

"Good, then I won't have to pussyfoot around."

"That's right."

I looked under all the mascara and tried to catch a glint that'd tell me what she was feeling, but found nothing.

"One other thing," I said as she walked me to the door. "Where were you last Wednesday night?"

"Right here. The whole evening."

I faced her a moment at the door, still trying to find something under all that stuff around her eyes that'd tell me if she resented the question or was suffering from any grief because of Felton's death. It didn't occur to me until I was halfway down the walk that if she showed any expression at all, it was amusement.

▽

8

SINCE FRYKMAN WAS PAYING the tab I went downtown
from the funeral parlor, picked a fair hotel, and got a room
some bigger than any at the Wilcox Hotel in Corden. This
one faced the street on the third floor and had rosy wallpaper,
a brown carpet covering most of the floor, and a fine blue
spread on the double bed. All it needed was a warm partner.

A few minutes after five Agatha opened her front door and
let me trail her up the steps, admiring her ankles all the way.
Evidently she'd ditched the etiquette book for the evening.

Her dress was red, and classier than the one she'd worn
earlier. The dining-room table was handsomely set for two
and it began to dawn on me she was after something. I
doubted it was my body or soul.

She made two whiskey drinks, mine with water, hers with
ginger ale.

"Okay," she said when we were settled in her living room,
"tell me about Carl Wilcox."

Most people I meet near Corden already think they know
too much about me, so it was nice to tell the lies for myself
once. But pretty soon, what with her steady gaze and smart
questions, I wound up telling her some of the truth. If she
was bunking me she was good enough to make it worth-

while. I even admitted I'd memorized some of Omar Khayyám and it turned out we knew several of the same verses, like the one about the moving finger and the checkerboard of nights and days.

Eventually we got around to my visit with Mrs. Clint and what she'd said and held back. I could see Agatha was disappointed her rival hadn't made a more elaborate attack on her. It suggested she wasn't taken seriously.

"What'd you think of her?" she asked. "What's she like?"

"Cagey. Gets what she wants and mostly keeps it."

"You think she's attractive?"

"About like a tiger."

She liked that and went to get us another drink. When she returned she sat beside me on the couch.

"You talk now," I said. "You've got a great voice."

That won me a warm smile and she asked what'd I want to know about—her fourth-grade class, teaching techniques, and discipline problems?

"How about where you come from, went to school, family—"

She leaned back. "I was born on a farm west of Wahpeton—that's North Dakota, not far over the border. Went to a country school, grew up spoiled as the only child of a young mom and an old dad. Dad gave up farming during the war and we moved to Edenberg, where eventually I got a teaching certificate at Edenberg Normal, went back, and taught in the school I went to as a kid. After two years of that I married a farmer. He was killed by his new tractor and I went back to teaching. Life story. Very dull."

"Tell me about the farmer. What was he like?"

"Jamie was sweet. Almost unreal. Not like any other man I've ever known. He thought I was perfect most of the time and spoiled me just like Mom and Dad did. Too good to last, I'm afraid."

She tried to keep that light, but her voice got thick.

"So Felton was quite a change."

"I suppose, in a way, I was looking for that. But I can't

believe I let myself waste so much time on a man like Felton.
Maybe it was something stupid, like being afraid to really
fall in love again. What I'm afraid of is I'm going to spend
the rest of my life falling in love with students that go away
and forget me. I really love little kids. My big ambition is to
teach first grade again. That's wonderful. The trouble is,
thinking of them growing up in this state, scrabbling for a
living all their lives, watching the wind blow the soil
away . . ."

She was sliding into a mood that makes women easy. As
I began thinking maybe I wouldn't need the hotel room, she
hopped up, said the chicken must be done, and rushed off
to the kitchen.

The dinner was almost good enough to make up for the
letdown. She laid out the works, with dumplings, mashed
potatoes, gravy, and a bird tender and juicy as a tramp's
dream.

Eating cheered her up, making her look younger than ever.
Her skin was the kind you can't imagine wrinkling, all
smooth and glowing. Her wide mouth was made for kissing.

"What'll you do next?" she asked as she poured coffee,
after we'd finished the chicken and brownies.

I guessed it'd depend on her, but said I wasn't sure.

"It'd help," I said, "if I had any lead on what kind of deal
Felton was into. Everything I've heard about him makes me
think he was ripe for a con game. You think he might've tried
to blackmail Mrs. Clint?"

She gave that some thought and reluctantly granted it
wasn't out of the question.

"It's embarrassing to admit how much bad I knew about
him. Every time he'd be gone a while I'd think of all the
reasons I shouldn't have had anything to do with him. Then
he'd come around, smiling and sweet, full of crazy stories
and big ideas, and I'd think this time'll be different, he's
really a good person and everything'll be lovely. That'd last
about a week. He was real good at making me feel anything
wrong between us was my fault."

That was a talent a high percentage of people I knew had. "Did he have any family around?"

"You know, it's strange when I think about it. He never talked to me about his parents or relatives. Not once. He brought up his dead wife when I first met him but never again. I think he used her to get sympathy—I know I felt he was a tragic figure when I first met him. She died of some awful disease. In some weird way that made me tolerate him, I guess."

She was silent a moment and suddenly smiled at me. "You know, this evening I've told you more about me than anybody I've known in Edenberg. You're very easy to talk to. You make a person feel you honestly want to know everything because you care."

"It's not an act."

"No, I'm sure it isn't. You genuinely like women, don't you? I mean, you're not just on the make. I can tell. You even liked that Clint woman. You didn't pick up on it real strong when I was snotty about her. Felton, if he'd got the standoff attitude from her you did, he'd have said she was a lesbian. Let's leave the table and go sit in the living room, okay?"

She told me to take the easy chair by the bookshelves, and parked in another a few feet to my left. As I took out my fixings and rolled a smoke she smiled.

"When I was a little girl my dad taught me how to work one of those gadgets that you make cigarettes with. I was very proud when I finished enough to fill the little case he carried. The doctor made him quit smoking after he got old and sick and the last thing he asked for was a cigarette. My mother was afraid to give it to him and to this day she feels guilty about not making him happy that last hour."

When the coffee was finished she apologized and said she'd have to ask me to leave because she had to be up early.

At the door she gave me her hand, then her mouth. Both were hot. I squeezed her more than was proper and when she felt the reaction she pulled away a little and patted my face.

"You're very nice, Carl. Thanks for coming. How long'll you be in town?"

"A couple nights like this and I might never leave."

I let her pull free and for a moment we stood grinning at each other.

"Keep in touch," she said, and closed the door.

▽

9

I WALKED FOUR BLOCKS along the quiet street to the business district and found it peaceful. Farmers don't spend Saturday nights in towns so big they can't be sure of running across friends in any store or restaurant they visit and where the local population is big enough to buffalo them.

I drifted into a beer joint and lifted one, hoping to talk with the bartender, but he was too busy to catch. When I looked up at the mirror behind the bar I met the eyes of an old-timer sitting to my right. He squinted at me.

"How'd it happen?" he asked me in the mirror.

"The nose?"

He nodded.

"Slingshot. Actually a rock from one. That was just the first time."

"You a fighter?"

"Not for pay."

"Look like one. A loser."

"You don't look like a champ yourself."

He grinned. His teeth were stained but even, and all present as far as I could see.

"Like they say, I'm a lover, not a fighter. You a stranger in town?"

"I know some people here."

"Like who?"

"Dick McCoy."

He turned from the mirror and looked at me straight. "No kidding? I wouldn't think you'd travel in the same circles. How'd you come to know Big Dick?"

"We both started in Corden."

"I be damned. He always talks like he come from maybe the Twin Cities or more east."

He grinned again, dug a pack of cigarettes from his shirt pocket, and offered me one. I took it. We lit up and kept looking at each other. I decided he wasn't as old as I'd first figured. His face was round and his nose broad, with dark hairs sprouting from the wide nostrils.

"You know McCoy pretty well?" I asked.

"Everybody knows McCoy," he said. "Old Big Dick, we call him."

I squinted against the smoke and told him for a lover he sure talked like a man who'd have to fight a lot.

He lifted a hammy paw and made an innocent face. "Hey, no offense, brother. Just kidding. McCoy's big stuff in our town. If he's your pal, you're lucky. In on the ground floor, as they say."

"You know a salesman worked for him? Felton Edwards?"

"He another friend of yours?"

"Never met him. Heard some things. What do you know?"

"I know he's dead. Was the tallest man in Edenberg, maybe the whole damned state. And hornier'n a billy goat."

"Know any of his friends?"

"Didn't have any. Not guys, anyway. Girls, that's another story."

"Where'd he drink?"

"Over at Summers' Bar. He liked Harriet. She owns the joint. They chinned a lot."

He said Summers' was across the street and south half a block. I thanked him for the cigarette, drank my beer, and drifted.

Summers' Bar was long and narrow with booths on each side for a ways beyond the entrance, then the bar on the right and more booths for four in a line straight to the rear wall, where the Ladies and Gents signs hung over two doors and Private over a third.

I ordered a beer from a husky who looked like he doubled as the bouncer, and rubbernecked around. A chunky woman with golden hair and a tight dress stood talking with four guys in a booth. The husky behind the bar took a sip from what looked like a glass of water and the next second the woman was reaching for it. He flushed and handed it over and she took a sniff, then a sip. She handed it back. Her voice was too low for me to hear but the man turned a deeper red and walked toward the end of the bar, untying his apron. The woman met him, took the apron, and returned his glare with a blacker one. He passed through the Private door and disappeared. The woman tied on the apron and began serving.

When she came near me I asked her how she could be sure the sacked bartender wouldn't smash things up on his way out the back. She scowled.

"He's stupid, but he's not an idiot. You want a refill?"

I nodded, got it, and watched her move off.

Half an hour later a replacement bartender relieved the boss lady, who gave him her apron and moved out among us once more. As she passed behind me I turned and asked if she'd give me a second.

She looked me over and said she wasn't hiring.

"I'm not looking. Want to talk about Felton Edwards. You know what happened to him?"

Her eyes narrowed. "Yeah."

A guy in a booth behind her hollered for a waiter and she turned to him quickly.

"Take it easy, Frank, you got the best waiter in the joint but he's busy, so just coast, okay?"

She smiled but her voice was heavy and the guy turned sheepish and nodded meekly.

"So what's Felton to you?" she asked, moving closer.

"I'm trying to find out why he was killed."

"What's it to you?"

"It's my job."

She tilted her head back. "You're pretty small for a private eye."

"You don't look like a bartender either."

"I know how."

"That's the way it is with me. I hear you talked with Felton a lot. Any idea why he pulled out of Edenberg six months ago?"

"Women and money."

"Women?'

"Yeah. He got overinvolved. And anyway, this burg was too small for him. Felton was a big man with big ideas."

"I heard he was planning to open a string of bars."

"Yeah. I told him he was nuts. Nobody owns more'n one saloon. Can't cover more. Guys behind the bar'd rob you blind. Goddamnedest vultures alive."

"Did Felton ask you to invest in his idea?"

She nodded and watched the new barman.

"You said no dice?"

"Bet your ass."

"Know anybody else he tried?"

"Les Clint."

"You know him?"

"Everybody knows Les. Our favorite undertaker."

"Where's he now?"

"Minneapolis, I think."

"Did he know about Felton and his wife?"

Her attention switched from the bartender to me and her eyes glinted. Her mouth was so narrow I figured one lipstick'd last her years.

"You been getting around, I guess. Who told you about that?"

"Everybody I've talked to so far except Pauline. She claims Felton was just a good friend."

"I should have such friends. Did Les know? Beats me. He's

not stupid but then again, he's not the swiftest. You deal with the dead, you get slow, I guess."

She didn't know any relatives Felton had around, said she'd always thought he was an orphan.

I asked if she remembered any guys Felton talked with often in the bar and she said there were maybe a couple. One was named Maxie. She didn't know his last name. I asked her to describe him. She said he was round-faced, chunky, and a kidder.

"With black hairs coming out his nose?"

"Yeah, you know him?"

"He sent me here."

"No kidding? That character. Probably knew Felton better'n anybody else in town. And he sloughed you off on me. Just like him."

I thanked her, finished my beer, and went back to the first bar. Maxie was gone, and no one I talked to knew when he'd left or where he went.

$\triangledown$

10

THREE BARS AND THAT many beers later I had exhausted
the town's supply of joints without locating Maxie and
returned to Summers' Bar.

The crowd had thinned with the witching hour on hand,
and I had no trouble cornering Harriet. She huddled with
two of her waiters and found one who knew Maxie's address
and another who said his last name was Hicks.

Maxie Hicks lived in an apartment on the third floor of
the Spriggs Block, a three-story square building with shops
on the ground floor and apartments above. I'd have thought
he'd pick a place over a bar.

The street entrance was three steps up and inside I
climbed a wide, fairly well-lit stairway. There was no halfway
landing, and it must've been a tough haul for fat Maxie. On
the second floor I paused, looked down the wide hall, then
turned right and started up the next flight. Halfway along I
smelled smoke, which goosed me into taking steps two at a
time, and as I popped up on the third level smoke puffed out
from under the nearest door on the left. The door number
was 301—Maxie's. I jumped for it and started hammering.
A woman in a wrapper shoved her door open down the hall
and screamed at me to knock it off.

"Fire!" I yelled. "Call help and get out!"

"Oh my God!" she cried, and disappeared.

I stepped back, kicked the door, and about broke my heel. It was solid as a safe. My second kick made it give and the third snapped the lock, slamming the door open and back against the inside wall. Smoke poured out, driving me back. Flames licked through the billowing clouds while I coughed and blinked my watering eyes.

I gave Maxie up and ran down the hall, hammering on doors and yelling fire, then raced down to the second floor and did the same routine.

Everybody anyone in the crowd knew about was down in the street by the time the fire trucks arrived. Everybody, of course, but Maxie Hicks. Firemen with smoke masks made a try for him, but gave up when they couldn't get through the flames. A neighbor said he'd probably fallen asleep drunk with a cigarette.

The lady who'd seen me kicking in Maxie's door gave me credit for saving them all and told the firemen, who told the police, and of course I wound up at City Hall in the morning answering questions from the chief who was very interested in why I just happened by at the time I did.

I laid out my story, which even sounded a little fishy to me. When he started turning hostile I decided the hell with secrets and told him to call Mayor Frykman in Hope. He wasn't at all impressed that I knew the number, but picked up the phone and made the call.

As far as I could see, the chief didn't like Frykman's story much more than mine, so I suggested he could check me out with Lieutenant Baker in Aquatown.

I didn't know that number but he got it quick enough, and of course found Baker off on Sunday. Sergeant Wendtland, Baker's favorite cop, confirmed that they knew me, I'd been the town cop in Corden once, and I hadn't been in jail or prison any time in the last five years. That last observation didn't exactly establish me as a sterling character in the chief's eyes. He suggested Wendtland locate Baker and ask him to call.

I suppose I should've been happy they didn't stick me in a cell but it galled me when they said hang around. There was nothing to read but wanted posters and a newspaper from the day before.

By noon Baker still hadn't called, so a fat cop named Peterson suggested we go across the street for lunch.

I got a tough beef sandwich and he ordered a hamburger with a chocolate malt. While he was chomping and slurping I asked what he could tell me about Maxie.

"Oh, he died. Didn't burn. Smoke done it."

"How'd the fire start?"

"Don't know yet. Probably a cigarette."

"What'd he do for a living?"

"Not much. His old man, called himself Manfred, left him money. Now Manfred, there was a guy! Whooee! Started out cardsharping when he was just a tad, made good money. Most gamblers just piss it away, but old Hicks worked the suckers and piled it up till he could work up a magic show, got himself a big tent and folding benches, and worked all around the Midwest. When the crash come it didn't hurt him none because he'd never trusted banks or stocks and stuff. Probably hid his wad in a sock. Anyways, Maxie was his only heir. Wife died way back. Maxie just wandered around town, talking to people, hittin' the speakeasies in Prohibition days and the bars when it went."

"You know Felton Edwards?"

"The tall gink? Saw him around. A guy that high, you can't miss 'im. Great bullshitter. Ran the dance hall awhile and peddled insurance for Dick McCoy. Ol' Big Dick."

"They call McCoy that because of the way he was hung or the action he got into?"

"Couldn't prove it by me. I never saw him hang it out and didn't keep track of his girling. None of my business."

"Ever hear why Felton left town six months ago?"

"Some say he'd laid all the women and sold insurance to all that'd buy so he just moved on to fresh territory."

"You say McCoy's a stud. Did he and Felton ever go after the same woman?"

"Who knows? If you're through we better get back. Chief'll wonder what the hell I'm doing. This is Dutch treat, you know."

The chief met us at the front door and told me I was on my own.

"You talked with Baker?"

"Yeah. You just take a hike, check out of your hotel, and go back to Hope. We'll handle things here."

"Baker didn't recommend that."

"I don't need Baker or Mayor Frykman telling me my business, and I sure as hell don't need you. So drift."

I thanked him for his hospitality, went back to the hotel, and telephoned Agatha from the lobby phone booth. She said she'd heard about the fire and they'd mentioned me as the man who got all the people out safely. I told her the police chief was so grateful he wanted to run me out of town but I figured maybe I could put it off till after I'd had dinner with her if she was interested.

She said she'd never dined with a hero before and would start today. We made a date for five-thirty.

When I left the booth and went for my key the desk man told me a newspaperman had been looking for me, and left a number I could call. I took it and did.

His name was Randolph Paxton and he wanted to know why I'd been in the Spriggs Block so late the night before.

"I was looking for Maxie Hicks. Somebody told me he knew a man I was trying to learn about."

He interrupted to ask if we could get together. I said fine.

We met in a small café with a counter and four booths. He was young with hollow cheeks, a sharp hooked nose, and moderate buckteeth. He probably expected a bigger hero, but had the grace not to show any disappointment.

He asked who was the guy I wanted to ask Maxie about.

I told him. His brown eyes bulged a little. "That the man murdered in Hope a couple days ago?"

"Yup."

"You some kind of cop?"

"No. I'm doing some checking up for a guy in Hope. Let's leave his name out, okay?"

"You're a private investigator."

I nodded.

"Okay. So whoever shot Edwards set fire to Hicks's apartment, right?"

"Nobody knows yet."

"But it looks like arson, right?"

I admitted I'd smelled smoke.

He laughed and didn't quite squirm with excitement.

I asked if he could find out anything about Maxie Hicks. Like if he had a bank account or any close friends.

He said he'd already tried. He knew from one of his people that Maxie lived off a trust, which kept him comfortable if not exactly flush. He'd been chummy with Felton, but as far as he knew the men had never had any common business interests.

He asked if I was going to be around a few days.

"Not if your town cop has his way, but maybe. There're still some people I want to talk with."

He wanted to know who and I stalled him off, saying I didn't have anything solid yet.

He gave me his home and work numbers and asked me to give him a call if I got any information he could use.

Back at the hotel, I called Frykman. He agreed the sign-painting job could wait, better I should stay in Edenberg. I told him that could be a problem since the local chief seemed set on running me out.

Frykman thought a moment, sighed, asked for the number I was calling from, and told me to sit tight, he'd be right back.

He wasn't that swift. I rolled and smoked two cigarettes while sitting in a rocker by the booth before he called.

"Okay," he said. "I've talked with Wally Berger, their mayor. He agrees with me that you can't be legally run out, and he'll tell his chief that. If the man gives you any further trouble tell him to talk with his mayor. Just stay there till you've learned all you can."

I didn't ask him what about.

$\triangledown$

11

THERE WAS NO ANSWER when I rang McCoy's number, but Agatha answered hers on the first ring.

"How about I pick you up early and we take a little ride?" I asked.

"You can't wait to see me, or you've got questions you want answered quick?"

"Both. The questions are, Why do you wear a girdle? and, Where's your favorite eating place?"

She sucked in her breath at the first question, gave a short laugh, and finally said she couldn't imagine how I knew since I'd not checked—

"Agatha, you wear one of those things and you can't tell if you've been touched. Where do you want to eat?"

"Decent women wear girdles, it's to keep from jiggling."

"What's wrong with jiggling?"

"It's provocative. I'd like to go to Eckerson's, a new place I've never tried."

She agreed I could pick her up at five, and we drove past the Spriggs Block where Maxie Hicks had died. I don't know a sorrier sight or smell than a burned building where people have lived. It was all black, and still wet because firemen kept at it so nothing'd bust loose and take fire again. It wasn't the kind of place where folks had owned anything fancy but all they had was gone and the loss was cruel.

I told Agatha I wished there was somebody around to tell me more about Hicks and she said a girlfriend had lived there a couple years back, what floor had Hicks been on?

"Third."

"So was my friend Bev. She's real friendly, maybe she got acquainted. Back then she was teaching sixth grade at my school. Then she married a dentist and had a baby."

We located a telephone booth and after a quick check through the directory Agatha called and got us invited to drop by after dinner.

Eckerson's wasn't cheap and Agatha was apologetic until I explained it'd be on my expense account. Then she ordered the beef roast, which was the dearest item offered. It wasn't bad but looked more tanned than cooked. She thought it was great even when I told her I'd seen beef get hurt worse than that and live.

She told me that a dentist was as close as Bev could come to marrying her ideal, which would've been a surgeon from the Mayo Clinic.

"We go way back together. In the fifth grade she told me she was going to marry a professional man. I didn't think that was snobbish then, it seemed like a dandy goal."

"What was yours?"

She shook her head as she cut her meat. "I never had any. For some reason I always thought things'd happen for the best. It didn't occur to me a person could choose a life and live it. Now that seems dumb, but let's face it, I haven't changed a bit."

"I thought maybe you wanted to marry the tallest guy in the state."

She wrinkled her ivory brow but took a moment of chewing before she spoke.

"I never thought of marrying Felton. That's an awful confession, but from the start I knew he was undependable and we'd never have a sweet little nest with bouncing babies and bliss. He hated kids. I couldn't tell him a thing about my darlings in the fourth grade. What was I doing to myself, being involved with such a man?"

She didn't expect an answer, and I didn't consider one.

"I wouldn't have been happy with Bev's dentist either. He's nice, but hopelessly limited. In some ways he's astonishingly ignorant. He heard how far away the moon is and got the idea it must be bigger than earth or we couldn't see it. I don't believe he's ever read a book in his life. Do you like kids?"

"Some."

"How about babies?"

"They buffalo me."

"That's what I'd expect. Don't worry, you won't have to hold Bev's."

She was right. By the time we got to the dentist's house the baby was asleep. We had to tippytoe into a dinky room they called the nursery and peek at the pink-cheeked little lump in the crib before returning to the living room for coffee.

Bev was a tall, slim brunette with gray eyes, high cheekbones, and not much nose. She was house-proud, babyproud, and not too ashamed of her hubby. He shook my hand with a bony, powerful grip and peered at my teeth with obvious professional interest.

"They look okay?" I asked.

He grinned and said they'd look better if I didn't smoke. I told him there was a limit to how much perfection became a man.

His name was Andrew Martin but everybody called him Doc. That's what Bev told us. He told me his friends called him Andy. We talked of weather, the meal, and the baby's perfection before getting around to Maxie. Then we had to go through sympathy for the loss and praise for the fire department, which had kept the blaze from wiping out a whole downtown block.

We learned Bev knew Maxie well. They'd met in the hall often and got on fine, particularly after Doc Martin fixed two cavities for him back when the couple was first going together.

"Maxie was an awful baby," said Bev. "When the new fillings gave him trouble he came to my door and I fixed him up with an ice pack and aspirin, and another time, when he had the flu, I called a doctor in and brought him soup and stuff. He was awfully appreciative so it was fun."

"Bev should've been a nurse," said Doc. "She loves fussing over people. If I were a really nice guy I'd come down sick once a month so she could take care of me."

"When's the last time you saw Maxie?" I asked Bev.

"About a week ago. I'd taken the baby downtown for a checkup and saw Maxie leaning over, talking to a man in a Packard. He seemed very interested."

"You see who was in the Packard?"

"Oh yes. You couldn't miss him even sitting in a car. It was Felton Edwards."

▽

12

SHE ADMITTED SHE HADN'T seen Felton's face clearly, but insisted the man had been too tall for anyone else. He had been around the Spriggs Block more than once, and she had assumed they were great cronies. Except for the time in the car she hadn't seen him in several months.

"Did Maxie talk about him?" I asked.

"Not a lot. I asked him if talking to somebody that tall gave him a kink in the neck and Maxie said no, he always asked him to sit down. You could tell Maxie liked him but he didn't go on about it."

"Felton figured he had money," said Doc confidently. "He was just cultivating him for a loan or investment deal."

"Did Felton ever ask you to invest in anything?" I asked him.

He laughed. "Nobody with sense'd be dumb enough to think a dentist'd have money. No. I never met the man."

When it was plain we weren't going to learn any more Agatha said she had to get to bed early, and I tried not to let myself believe that was promising as we got up to leave.

It wasn't. She didn't want to go anywhere and park and didn't invite me in because, as she explained, everybody in town would know if she had me up to her place two evenings in a row. She gave me a quickie kiss at the door and was gone.

Back at my hotel the clerk gave me my key and a note from McCoy asking me to call.

I used the lobby booth and a moment later a woman answered and called him to the phone.

His "Hello?" was so cautious and questioning I guessed right off the woman was his wife and she didn't know he expected the call. I gave my name.

"Oh, yeah, Wilcox. I thought you'd left town."

"Is that why you left a call for me?"

He laughed but it wasn't natural. "Well, uh, sure. How about I come around and pick you up—where are you?"

"Right where you left your message."

"Well, all right," he said heartily, "if it's that important I'll come around right away."

I said peachy, I'd wait out front.

His black Olds was all shiny under the streetlight and he shoved the door open as I approached. I slid in and he drove on.

We went several blocks, with him keeping his eyes on the gravel under his headlights, until we reached a dinky park where he pulled off to the side under a row of elms, killed the engine, and turned to me.

"I hear you took Mrs. Simpson to lunch yesterday. What was the point of that?"

"Several."

"Huh?"

"Points. One; she isn't half bad-looking and it seemed she'd be eating alone. Two; you hadn't been any help so I figured she might be. Three; I'm checking on a murder so it's my business to ask questions and, not being a cop, I couldn't just haul her into the station and work her over with a rubber hose. So what's your problem?"

He scowled sternly. "It looks bad, a man like you taking my secretary out in public like that."

"You think it'd been better if I'd taken her up to my hotel room?"

"You're not funny. You always thought you were and you've made plenty of fools laugh but you're not a goddamned bit funny."

"You are. You're a barrel of laughs. So why'd you want to talk to me?"

"I don't want you making me look bad. I carry some weight in this town, by God. You give me any trouble, you'll regret it."

"No shit? You got a law against taking widows to lunch?"

He glanced in the rearview mirror as a car approached from behind and sat stiff until it passed. Then he lowered his head, tilted it back, and took a deep breath.

"All right. I'm going at this bassackwards. I'll admit I'm upset. This goddamn thing with Felton scares me. People know he and I didn't get on the last year he worked for me. I know they're talking. Even my wife wonders—"

"What was the trouble?"

"Oh hell, all kinds. He was a constant pain. Helluvva salesman when he wanted but he wanted too damned little, and he antagonized other salesmen and was disrespectful to me. He made customers think he was their only friend in the company and nobody'd look out for their interests but him. And on top of that, all his womanizing. It was a scandal—"

"You two didn't happen to share a target, did you?"

"What makes you think that?" he demanded, turning toward me. "Who told you that?"

"I figured it out. It had to be something like that for you to get in a panic and want to see me on a Sunday night. I'd guess your secretary, Lois, is the one. Right?"

"Lois? Lois Simpson? That's ridiculous. Of course not!"

"Too bad. She's all right, you know. Loyal as hell. But I suppose the problem's a younger one."

"There's no problem like that. The silly bastard was giving my company a bad name, that's all. I told him to goddamn straighten up or get out and he got out. And then he had the gall to come back and ask me to invest in a harebrained notion of building a tavern in town. Said if I didn't he'd go around to his old customers and tell them things about insurance and me."

"He came to see you? When?"

For a second he looked confused. Then he frowned and shook his head.

"No, he telephoned. He couldn't make a pitch like that in my office. And it was months ago—"

"What month?"

"Eh? Oh, about six. Right after he quit and left town."

"What'd he have to say to your customers that'd give you trouble?"

"A lot of nonsense about Lois and me. Goddamnit, why aren't you looking for Les Clint? He's the guy Felton Edwards was screwing. He's the logical suspect."

"You know Polly pretty well?" I asked.

"Not that well. I know about anybody who's anybody in town but I've got better sense than to screw around with clients' wives, especially ones that're loaded."

He started to unwind and admitted at one time he and Felton had been pals. That was when Felton first came to work for him and made McCoy believe they'd both get rich. They'd drunk together, exchanged life stories, attended American Legion meetings—

"What'd he tell you of his family?"

"They came from New York State. Lived in North Dakota when he was a kid. His ma died having another kid that was stillborn and his old man died of flu while Felton was in the army. Felton served in France but never saw any action. Claimed they didn't put him in combat because he was too big a target. He was an MP in Paris."

I thought he'd have seen some combat if he'd been MPing the night I kicked one of his kind into the Seine. God knows I saw plenty action that evening.

I asked if Felton had talked about marriage. He said no.

We sat in silence for a while before he sighed again and

said he guessed he'd better get me back to the hotel. During
the short drive he was silent, but as we pulled up in front of
the hotel he glanced at me.

"Do me a favor, okay? Leave Lois Simpson alone."

"I got all I expect to from her."

"She's a fine woman," he said. "I don't want anything bad
to happen to Lois."

"It won't come from me."

He nodded distractedly as he peered up and down the
empty street and asked how long I'd be in town.

"No longer than I have to. If you could tell me somebody
else who knew Felton real well, it might help."

"Try Harriet Summers. She runs Summers' Bar. She sure
as hell saw enough of him."

"She got a husband?"

"Not anymore. He was shot in a mob thing during Prohibition. She took over the speakeasy and made the conversion
when Roosevelt freed the liquor crowd."

"She got a boyfriend?"

"I hear one of the bartenders is close, but I'm not sure.
She's independent as a hog on ice."

"What's the guy's name?"

"Cotton Mather."

"I thought he was dead."

"I guess the original is. This one's sure as hell no Puritan
preacher."

I got out of his car, went to bed, and thought about Cotton
Mather the first. It put me to sleep quick.

▽

13

I WOKE MONDAY THINKING of all the great women I'd got nowhere with in the past week and wondering if premature old age had taken off my edge. It sure wasn't for lack of want. Going to the toilet down the hall eased the pain but not the ache and after a shave and a washup I headed out, looking for breakfast.

The day was bright, the sky pale blue promising hot, and a lazy breeze puffed dust along the paved main street. A few folks were astir and I even saw a couple cars go by but there was none of the frantic you see in a town like Minneapolis.

I entered a café that advertised breakfast with a sloppy sign on a card in the window and thought maybe I'd ought to drum up some business but decided I owed full-time to Frykman at this stage. I could always come back when this job ended.

The counterwoman wasn't the type to get my ache started again, but of course I didn't have sense enough to feel grateful. The service was good, the waffles fine, and the bacon crisp enough to crackle. I worked through it all with lots of coffee, rolled a smoke, and eyed the place.

There was a phone booth beside the men's-room door and when I'd finished my smoke I went over, fed it a nickel, and

got the operator to ring Leslie Clint's number. After a while
a woman answered. It wasn't Polly. I asked for Mr. Clint.

"He's not home."

"Still out of town?"

"Who's calling?"

I told her. She said yes, Mr. Clint was still out of town. I
asked for Mrs. Clint. She wasn't available.

"How about you, are you available?"

That brought a giggle.

"I'd like to come out and talk with you," I said, "okay?"

"About what?"

"What you do, what you'd like to do. You're Norse, right?"

"How'd you know that? I haven't got a accent."

"You sing when you talk."

"Oh, ya." She giggled again.

"I'll be around in a bit."

She said okay.

The rising prairie wind felt warm and smelled of straw
and dust. A younker pushed a heavy mower over the funeral
home's lush lawn and the smell of new grass drove away the
prairie as I approached the family door. It took a few seconds
before the maid appeared and she was just as I'd pictured
her: apple-cheeked, snub-nosed, blond, and freckled. She
gave me a broad grin and stood behind the screen with her
arms folded under plump breasts.

"You're younger than you sound," I said.

"You're older."

"You win that one. Is Mrs. Clint home?"

"Huh-uh."

"You mean not to me?"

"I mean she's not home."

"So you won't let me in?"

"Ya, that's right."

I asked for her name and she said it was Signa, emphasiz-
ing the *a*. In response to questions she said she was a
farmer's daughter from near Doland and had been working
for the Clints almost six months. I asked if they ever had a

visitor named Felton Edwards. She said no, but sounded uncertain.

"They talk about him?"

She shrugged. Either the grin was a permanent fixture or my face was unusually amusing. The grin kept getting wider.

When I scowled at her she giggled, bringing both hands up to her pink face.

"What's cracking you up?" I asked.

"You. You're real funny."

"I always thought so but mostly I have to work at it. How come it's so easy with you?"

The lawn mower had stopped not long after I began amusing the maid and I saw the younker come around the corner of the house, scowling. He was a head taller than me, with bony shoulders, a jutting jaw, straw-colored hair, and huge hands. He stopped about three paces away.

I took him in and asked Signa if this was her boyfriend.

If she thought I was funny before she found me hilarious now. The mower guy wasn't at all amused.

"Whaddaya want?" he demanded.

"What've you got?"

"Signa's supposed to be doin' the wash, not gabbin' with bums."

"She'll get it done. Why don't you go push your mower?"

He stuck his chin out. "Don't tell me what to do. Just get on your way—we don't feed bums."

Good sense should have told me to bow out but I never have good sense in front of a woman when a man puts me down. I told him to get lost.

His first punch came quick and straight and told me he'd fought before and was probably older than he looked. I ducked, hooked him in the gut, and jerked my head up as his came down. My noggin caught him between the eyes. The crack showed me stars and laid him out cold.

When I looked up at the screen the maid's grin was gone and her mouth formed an **O**.

"I guess he is your boyfriend," I said.

She opened the door, darted out, and knelt over him, clucking in alarm. His eyes opened and his legs twitched. He saw her, blinked, shook his head, and managed to focus on me. That got him starting up, but Signa grabbed him and told me to go away.

As I started turning away Polly Clint showed up in the doorway and told her maid to take Herman into the kitchen and give him some lemonade. The couple got organized and went past her sheepishly. She regarded me like a school-teacher taking in a naughty boy.

"I really ought to call the police," she said.

"He started it." I grinned.

"What'd you expect to learn from her?"

"Not much. I was hoping to smoke you out."

She glanced left, right, and over my head, pushed the screen open, and told me to come in. I followed her into the living room and sank into an easy chair. She sat dead-center on the couch and studied me with her slanty eyes.

"You said you were home last Wednesday evening. What time did your husband leave?"

"I don't know for sure. A little after supper. We had a small quarrel and I was up in my room when he left. I didn't hear him go."

"Didn't he have to pack?"

"We have our own rooms."

I thought about that while she watched me.

"Heard from your husband since he left?" I asked.

"No."

"When you expect him back?"

"When he gets here."

"What'd you quarrel about?"

"I don't think that's any of your business, but I've nothing to hide. He wanted me to go to the city with him. I am bored to death by undertakers and said no."

A telephone rang somewhere and the second ring was cut off midway. She stirred nervously, and I guessed she was trying to hear what the maid was saying down the hall.

"Have you heard about another man being murdered?" I asked.

She frowned irritably and said no.

"Guy named Maxie Hicks. Friend of Felton's. Know him?"

She shrugged. "I doubt it. I don't pretend to know all the people Felton knew."

"Want to tell me what your husband's doing in Minneapolis?"

"He's attending an undertakers' convention and visiting with our daughter, who's at the university there."

"In the summer?"

"Yes. She got sick during finals this spring and missed exams, so she's doing makeup."

"Did she know Felton?"

The slant eyes narrowed. "Why do you ask that?"

"I hear Felton liked them young."

"That's ridiculous. No, she didn't know him—she met him here, I suppose—but they never—"

I asked for the daughter's name. She said it was Elaine.

"Got any other kids?"

"A boy. He's at Missouri. Wants to be a journalist, of all things." She tried to make light of that but the pride was clear. I hadn't caught any similar feeling about the daughter. His name, she told me, was Richard but everyone called him Sonny. He was a top student.

I didn't think Sonny would be any help to me but I was sure I should go to Minneapolis. If my ear was good, mama was jealous of her daughter.

▽

14

I WALKED UNDER BOX elders and elms lining the street to the hotel and read a day-old newspaper in the lobby. The only good news was on the funnies page, where Little Orphan Annie and Daddy Warbucks triumphed again.

Since the desk clerk had no messages for me I made a call on my own.

A few minutes later I was talking with Logan, the Minneapolis cop who'd once invited me never to darken his town again. Later we'd become almost buddies.

He gave me his usual baloney before settling down to hear my story.

"I want to know if there was an undertakers' convention in Minneapolis last weekend—and, if so, where was it?"

"If nobody was robbed or shot at this shindig, why'd I know anything about it?"

I told him he knew everything and he said that was a surprise to him but if I said so it must be true and asked me to wait a minute.

A moment later he said, "You're right, I do know everything. Like there's an undertakers' bash but it starts tomorrow and it's at the Radisson. You getting into a new line?

Figure after all your experience with stiffs you'd ought to make some money off them?"

"An undertaker's wife told me her hubby was there for the meeting. This wife's boyfriend got shot in a town near here Wednesday night. Isn't that interesting?"

"I'd say you got yourself a hot clue, Wilcox. You want I should find out if this citizen's got a reservation for the powwow here?"

"I do. I'll call back this afternoon, okay?"

"Fine. You're gonna owe me one, you know."

"I'll send you a Christmas card."

He laughed and hung up.

After lunch I went around to Summers' Bar. It was pretty dead, but the latter-day Cotton Mather was on duty. Nothing about him suggested a puritan. His voice had the timbre of a well-whiskied larynx and his smile was shamrock Irish. The red hair around his dome was too thin to hide his skull but along the sides it became bushy enough to half-hide his big ears. When I ordered a draft he drew it so smooth and easy he hardly seemed to move before the glass was on the bar before me.

"I hear you knew Felton Edwards," I said.

He glanced at me side-eyed, and the bright grin faded a few watts. "Any bartender in this territory knew Felton," he assured me.

"He ever tell you about the tavern he was gonna build?"

The grin turned up again. "Felton's Finest? You bet. I'd guess every bartender in South Dakota heard about it and was promised a job one day."

"I guess you didn't believe him?"

"When it comes to faith, friend, I reserve it for God and even there, I've wee doubts."

"Wee? That's not Irish."

"I'm only half. The other's Scotch and English."

"We're practically brothers," I told him, "except I've some French snuck in the line somewhere. So the tavern builder never really named anybody putting money in the plan?"

"Well," he winked broadly, "there was a hint now and again that a certain lady's husband might pop. If he didn't find out first the lady'd been diddling with Felton."

"If Les didn't know that already, he must've been the only man in town who didn't."

"That's the way it goes."

"When'll your boss lady be in?"

"Around supper."

After finishing my beer I called Logan in Minneapolis. He was out but had left a message. Leslie Clint was registered for the meeting.

I telephoned Frykman and told him I should go to Minneapolis to pursue the investigation. He told me kindly that he didn't think that a prudent investment and suggested I return to sign-painting. He suspected I'd already run up a hefty bill.

That deflated me some. After lunch I dropped by Summers' Bar, got Harriet's home address from Cotton, and walked over. She lived in a two-story white house on a treeless lot facing south and answered my knock promptly. The golden hair looked some strawish in sunlight and her complexion was mottled but unusually smooth, with only small wrinkles around her eyes and mouth.

"Well," she said, returning my stare, "you planning to do a portrait?"

"You willing to sit?"

"Why not? But if you draw me ugly I'll kill you."

"I can't even draw stick men," I confessed. "How about we talk a little?"

She pushed the screen open and preceded me down a hall and through a door on the left to her living room. It was neat and spare. No doilies, dainty tables, fancy vases, or knickknacks, just solid brown leather chairs and a broad matching couch. The carpet was mixed-up browns, mostly dark. The pictures I can't remember.

"One of the people I talked with said you probably knew

Felton better than you let on to me," I said.

"Yeah? How well's that supposed to be?"

"Better than most."

"Better than his two paramours?"

It surprised me she knew the word. I wasn't sure I did.

"My information's not that particular."

"We talked. That's all we did. I'm not a horizontal lady in the social way. Besides he was too damned big for a little lady like me and what kind of a broad do you take me for?"

"I take you for a woman who does as she pleases and that's the best kind. All I want is to find out if you know anybody who'd have a good reason to kill the man."

She sat in her chair too straight to be natural, watching me as if I might make a sudden move to grab her and she was fully prepared to flatten me if I tried.

Suddenly she settled back. "I might have."

"Why?"

"He called me a lesbian."

"What brought that on?"

"I belted him when he patted me on the ass."

"That doesn't seem quite enough to make you shoot him."

She scowled. "For me, it doesn't take much."

"What kind of a gun did you use?"

She threw back her head and laughed.

"Okay," she said, "so I'm bullshitting you. I haven't got a gun, never owned one. The only ones I know might've killed him are Polly's husband, that schoolteacher he dumped, and McCoy. There are probably half a dozen other horned hubbies around the state that aren't in mourning now he's dead."

"Why'd McCoy have it in for him?"

"Oh hell, everybody knows they scrapped for years. It sort of reached a head when they both got hustling that biddy in McCoy's office."

I asked if there were any other names she knew that I didn't.

"Well, there was a guy named Gus who came in once, looking for Felton. Actually came around twice. Both times Felton wasn't around. When I asked Felton after the first time if he knew this Gus he said it was just some sap he'd horned and if he came around he'd beat the bastard's ears off."

"When was Gus in last?"

"A few months ago. Come to think of it, probably a couple after Felton left town. I don't guess the guy really wanted to find him."

"What do you know about this Gus?"

"Only what Cotton told me. That he was a plow jockey named Rasmussen and lived on a farm somewhere between Corden and Hope."

Well, well.

$\bigtriangledown$

15

COTTON GAVE ME GENERAL directions to Rasmussen's farm, which worried me some since there were no gas stations on the prairie and too many wrong turns might leave me with an empty tank. Everything worked out fine after I stopped and got detailed directions from a farmer. When country folk say a place is two miles east and three quarters of a mile south you can bet that's right within inches.

Rasmussen's farm was dry as the rest but a sight neater. Wind, dust, sun, and cold had whipped the paint job to memories and the few miserable cows in his pasture were down to skin, bones, and tail tassels. His fences were still tight and there was no junk on the dried-up grass around the house. He might be losing his shirt but he hadn't lost his pride.

I wheeled up the rut road, turned off the engine, and sat a second, staring at the still house and the dust blowing across the field beyond. Wind rocked my car.

A figure appeared behind the battered screen on the side door. Farmers in our territory never use front doors for anything but funerals and weddings. I got out and started toward the house. No dog came to meet me. The last time I'd gone through this routine a farmer's wife had run me off with a shotgun and I hoped nothing like that was going to happen again.

"Afternoon," I called.

The woman behind the screen didn't answer.

"Is this the Rasmussen place?" I asked.

"Who wants to know?"

The voice was neither friendly nor hostile.

"Carl Wilcox. Looking for Gus Rasmussen. He home?"

"Near."

"I'd like to talk with him."

"What about?"

"Felton Edwards."

After a moment she asked if I was a detective.

I said I was investigating the man's death.

I couldn't be sure she caught the evasion. Her expression was hidden by the screen and shadows.

"Gus didn't have anything to do with it. He hasn't been off the farm in a week."

"I guess you're Mrs. Rasmussen."

She didn't think that was worth answering. I walked a little closer, slow and easy. Now I could see she stood with her arms folded tightly across her chest. She was tall, slender, and dark-haired.

"I'm the one you should talk to," she said at last. "You want to come in?"

I did and she led me into the kitchen, which was cool and square under a high ceiling. I glanced around at the sparse white cabinets, the black pump by the sink, and a big dark range. I could smell bread, coffee, and soap. A sturdy square table sat in the center, with two straight-backed spindle chairs tucked in facing each other. Their varnish was cracked and peeling.

I heard movement overhead and glanced at the woman, who paid it no attention, went over to the stove, turned, and stared at me.

She was younger than I'd guessed at first, probably no

more than mid-twenties. Her smooth pale face hadn't been worked over yet by summer sun or winter wind. Her slim, long-fingered hands were ruddy but unchapped. The house-dress gave nothing away about her body; it was loose, high at the collar, and low at the hem.

"How'd you meet Felton?" I asked.

"He sold insurance to Pap."

"When?"

"Fourteen years ago."

"What were you then, about eight?"

Her eyes widened and her chin lifted.

"How'd you know?"

"Only a guess," I admitted.

"You want to sit?" she asked, unfolding her arms. She was very small-breasted.

I said okay and did, thinking she'd be more comfortable looking down at me, but then she pulled out the facing chair and sat too.

There was a coffeepot on the stove, off to the side, so I guessed it was empty or too old to reheat. Again there was movement upstairs and again she ignored it.

"So you've known Felton a long time," I said.

"Yes."

"Like him?"

She folded her hands on the table, stared at them sadly, and nodded.

"Was he your lover?"

"He wanted to be," she said, not lifting her eyes.

"But you didn't let him?"

"Never."

"Sorry you didn't?"

She took a deep breath, looked at me, and released it in a sigh. "I'm afraid so—I don't know. He was crazy about me and now he's dead for nothing."

"You think Gus did it?"

"No. But everybody else will because he was stupid

enough to go in town and make big noises in a bar before everybody. It was so stupid! He knew Felton wouldn't be there but he pretended he was after him."

"Why're you so sure he didn't do it?"

"Because he wouldn't even hit me when he thought I'd flirted with Felton. He's never owned a gun and wouldn't know where to get one."

"Where was he Wednesday night?"

"Home," she said but she didn't look at me.

"Is that him upstairs?"

"No," she said, suddenly meeting my eyes. "That's Katie, my little girl. I sent her up when I saw your car."

"Would you call her down?"

"She doesn't know anything. Why'd you want to see her?'"

"I'd just like to."

"Oh," she said, making a face, "you don't believe me. You think it's Gus."

"I'd feel better if I could see her."

"She won't know if her father was home Wednesday night. She goes to bed early."

I promised not to ask the little girl any leading questions and, after giving me a look that suggested she was disappointed in me, she lifted her head and called the girl's name. I heard footsteps on the stairs, only a few, which indicated she'd already come halfway down. A moment later, a dark-haired girl of about four came into the kitchen. Her eyes were deep blue and round as a doll's. Her face was round too, although her body was slim, almost skinny. Her hair was bobbed short.

"This is Mr. Wilcox," her mother told her.

"Is he gonna fall in love with you?" asked Katie.

"What a thing to say!" said the mother. I wouldn't have believed that pale face could get such color.

"Papa says all men fall in love with Mama," Katie told me.

"He's probably right," I said. "She's very pretty. So are you."

"Thank you. I'm three and a half. What happened to your nose?"

"Katherine! What a thing to say!" The mother's face turned a marvelous scarlet.

"I put it in the wrong place a couple of times," I told Katie.

She thought of exploring that further but after a glance at her mother decided it wasn't safe.

"Let's have a cookie," she suggested.

That distraction brought Mrs. Rasmussen's complexion back to normal and a moment later we each had a glass of milk and a ginger cookie. The cookies were chewy and rich, the milk cold from the icebox.

"Where's Gus?" I asked.

"Working on the west fence. He wouldn't tell you anything I haven't. But I suppose you won't believe me."

"It's not a matter of believing," I told her. "The thing is, no one person knows the whole story about anything. When you get a deal like this, you can't leave any more blank spots than you have to."

She thought about that, said for me to wait, and went out and rang a triangle suspended outside the kitchen door.

"Where'd you put your nose?" Katie whispered.

"In front of a stone a boy sent from a slingshot," I whispered back.

Her eyes got bigger. "Did it hurt?"

"You bet."

She quit the questions when her mother returned, and wiped milk from her upper lip. As I finished my cookie footsteps sounded outside and then Gus came in.

"How old's your Model T?" he asked me before his wife could make introductions.

"Twelve years."

"Looks in good shape. What's the box on the running board for?"

"Painting stuff, bedroll, tools."

"You a housepainter?"

"I've done them. Mostly I do signs."

His wife gave me a bewildered look as he got a chair from another room, and then she brought him a glass of milk and a cookie.

"I don't guess," said Gus, "you came out here to try and sell me a sign."

"No. I'm doing a little work for Mayor Frykman, of Hope. He asked me to check out what happened to Felton Edwards."

"Why, he planning to pin a medal on whoever did it?"

Mrs. Rasmussen rose and said she and Katie were going up to the bedroom. Gus nodded without looking at her. His cold brown eyes stayed on me. When we were alone he leaned both elbows on the table.

"So what're you, a deputy? A sign-painting deputy?"

"I've been a cop in Corden."

"Oh." For once it seemed I'd found a man in my territory who never heard of Carl Wilcox. Like many farmers I'd met, his only real interest was in his farm; occasionally he remembered he had a family.

"I hear you went into Summers' Bar in Edenberg a while back and let them know you were looking for Edwards. You ever find him?"

He shook his shaggy head. "Wasn't even trying to. Just wanted to warn him off."

"That kind of warning doesn't make your wife look too good."

"Yeah, so she told me. I just got mad. Stupid mad."

"What'd you done if you found him?"

"Probably got my head punched in. That son of a bitch's jaw was out of my reach unless I carried along a baseball bat, and I didn't think of it at the time."

"Your wife says she'd known Edwards since she was a kid. What tripped the mad-on?"

"He came to see her when I was gone and made a pass. She told me about it. I went looking for him."

"At the bar they say you came around twice."

"He came here twice."

"What'd you done if you caught him in your house?"

"I'd have killed him—or tried."

"Did you?"

"Oh sure. Shot him with my .44, which I always wear except on Mondays. Did it right here in front of Katie. Then I hauled him in my Chevy to Hope, found a handy sandpit, and left him for the buzzards."

I drank a little more milk and studied him.

"Well?" he said.

"You think I could have another ginger cookie?"

$\triangledown$

16

Bᴀᴄᴋ ɪɴ Hᴏᴘᴇ I stopped for a late supper at Winkle's, and after delivering my hamburger and fries Mary hung around to ask where I'd been and what I'd been doing.

"Visiting old stomping grounds," I said.

"Got a girl, I bet."

"Not me. I took a vow."

"Uh-huh, and I'm gonna be sainted next Sunday."

Before we got beyond that Mayor Frykman came in, ambled our way, and told Mary to bring coffee. As she left he slipped into the booth bench across from me.

"I expected you earlier," he said.

"Stopped to visit a farmer someone in Edenberg told me had threatened Felton."

"Really?" His sad eyes brightened a little as he thanked Mary when she delivered the coffee. He waited until she was back in the kitchen before asking who.

I told him about Rasmussen and my visit at their farm.

"What'd you think?"

"Unlikely he did it."

He was disappointed, obviously hoping for assurance that the murderer was someone from outside his town.

He asked for details of my sessions with Edenberg people

and I started telling him of the rumors I'd picked up about
Felton and Dick McCoy, his boss at the insurance company,
getting into competition for the favors of the middle-aged
secretary. I told him about Gus Rasmussen's question as to
whether the killer would get a medal, and was pleased when
he seemed to appreciate the idea.

When a citizen walked past the front window and
squinted in at us Frykman got upset and started sliding out
of the booth.

"You come around to my place after dark," he said. "I
want a full report in private."

"Okay. I'd like a payoff on expenses to date—the hotel bill
about cleaned me out."

"Of course," he said, "I'll take care of it."

I took a swing past the Cole Hotel to check on mail or
calls and found none. Up in my room I changed my shirt
and socks and, since it'd be a while before dark, strolled over
to check out Mac McGillacuddy's aunt.

She was weeding in the garden with a piece of carpet under
her knees and her hair covered with a blue bandanna. She
started in surprise when I spoke, then smiled as she straightened and sat on her heels.

"Well," she said. "Mac's missed you."

"I hope he hasn't found any more bodies."

"Not yet. Is that why you came, to check on that?"

"No. I wanted to see you."

"I've already told you all I know."

"You haven't had the time to do that."

"So what're you after? Another cookie?"

"That's my big weakness."

"All right," she said, rising. "I'll get some, and tea."

"Where's Mac?"

"Off on his bike. Wait for me, I'll only be a moment."

I sat on the stoop and built a cigarette while staring at her
gardens. Off to the left a gopher's head poked up from a
clay-covered mound and bright black eyes stared at me a
moment. Then, with a flicker of his tail, he was gone.

When Florence returned she'd removed the bandanna and fluffed up her blond hair. I admired its glow as she set down the tea tray, poured for each of us, and took one of the white sugar cookies from a flowered plate.

Her smile broadened as she watched me butt out my cigarette, shred the end, and scatter it underfoot.

"For a naturally rough man," she said, "you're surprisingly neat. Were you in the army?"

"Yup. But the toughest first sergeant I ever had was Ma. You make great cookies."

"Grandma taught me how."

At this point we were getting on so fine it was awfully hard to think of spoiling it, but I had to ask.

"Everything I've heard about Felton Edwards says he was a guy with an eye for the ladies and, considering the size of Hope and the looks of the lady I'm with, I can't help thinking he must've come around sometime. Did he?"

She smiled. "You're amazing. You just get me thinking I've a suitor and suddenly let me know I'm being interrogated. Is it possible you're considering Officer Ruppman as a suspect in Felton's murder?"

"That's a pretty broad jump from my question."

"Not at all. I know Officer Ruppman well enough to guess he's warned you off, and it's not hard to go from there to guessing that you've decided the deceased tried to woo me and came to grief by it."

"Well, Ruppman *is* the only guy around who always carries a gun."

She drank tea while watching me over the cup rim. When she put it down she said, "If it was him, you'll be in something of a fix, won't you? Who're you going to report it to?"

"The mayor. Did Felton try for you?"

"Yes." Her smile was near as cozy as a good-night kiss.

"How far'd he get?"

"A good deal short of first base. I don't care for men that tall or irresponsible."

"I hear he tried for you before you went to Minneapolis. Did he try when you came back?"

"If he'd known where the stoop would be, he'd have been waiting at it when I arrived."

"Did you turn him down because of Ruppman?"

"I already told you, he wasn't my type."

"You didn't shoot him, did you?"

"No." For the first time since I'd arrived she didn't seem amused. "You're turning out to be a great disappointment, you know that?"

"I usually do," I admitted. "The fact is, I came around tonight because I wanted to see you, not thinking of the murder or anything else. Then I couldn't help thinking what a terrific woman you are and how funny it was you'd never been married and didn't seem to have a guy. It doesn't make sense."

"Haven't you heard that Mac's my son and he came from Johnnie Powers?"

I nodded.

"Do you believe it?"

"It sounded natural, yeah. All except the guy letting you go. He must be a dumb jerk."

"I like to think so. Whatever he is, he's not Mac's father. I would never have come up with such a long last name. And now Officer Ruppman looks after me."

"Does he move in?"

"No. He's very honorable, and I don't encourage him."

"Don't you feel caged?"

"Not as long as no one I want is bullied off."

I thought about that a little and wasn't sure where it left me.

"Let me help you," she said. "You haven't been frightened off, have you?"

"I've been warned."

"Well, obviously you weren't impressed. You're here."

"Yeah."

"And all it's got you is cookies and tea, that's what you're thinking, isn't it?"

"Hey, don't knock cookies."

She broke out in a really great laugh.

"You keep that up," I told her, "and you're gonna get kissed."

She did, and she was. I felt one of her hands pressing the back of my head firmly. She didn't open her mouth and I didn't try to force it because everything was just right and I wasn't going to spoil it again by moving too fast. When we came up for air she pressed her head against my chest and sighed.

The front door slammed. She pulled free and touched her hair.

"That's Mac," she said. "It's the first time I remember being grateful that he slams the door."

It was turning dark as we carried the tea stuff inside. Mac met us in the kitchen and gave me a studied look. I asked how things were going. He said okay. She gave him a cookie and we talked a little more.

When I left the two of them were watching me from the front door.

Ruppman waited until I was half a block from the hotel before pulling up beside me in his Model A. I took my hands out of my pockets and faced him as he climbed out of his car and started for me.

17

HE LOOKED BIGGER THAN I remembered as he lowered his head and hunched his shoulders.

"Hi," I said.

"Hi shit. I told you I didn't need any cop help. What the hell you think you're doing?"

"Right now I'm heading for Mayor Frykman's."

He halted. "You took a damned roundabout way."

"He didn't want me till after dark so I had some time to kill."

He glowered at me. It was quite dark now as we stood in the middle of the block between feeble intersection lights. A warm breeze stirred thin hair on his forehead. His hands dangled at his sides, the right one just under the gun at his hip.

"Okay," he said, "I can't keep Frykman from hiring you for whatever the hell he's got in mind, but keep your goddamn paws off Florence. You mess with her and it'll be your last woman."

I let that pass until he turned and went back to his car. When he slammed the door I leaned toward him.

"Is that what you told Felton?"

He was silent for a second. Then he chuckled.

"You're cute, Wilcox. You knew if you said that when I was in front of you that nose'd been busted again. I'm gonna have trouble with you, right down to the end."

"That's up to you."

"Yeah. Don't figure you can make Frykman believe I killed Felton. It wouldn't be convenient. Mayor Frykman's a man likes everything neat and clean. No embarrassments. You won't last."

He started the car and I listened to its lovely, rough purr before he stuck it in gear and drove off.

It took the housekeeper a while to reach Frykman's door when I knocked, and she greeted me with the same enthusiasm she showed the first time. I followed her down the hall past the big living room and found him at his whopping rolltop desk. He turned, frowning in thought, waved me to the easy chair, and put down a fountain pen he'd been writing with.

When I was settled and rolling a smoke he told me Officer Ruppman was very unhappy about me.

"He says you'll stir up everyone and take advantage of women in town. I know you've quite a reputation from the past but I've been assured by people who should know that your performance in recent years has been much improved."

I nodded.

He considered me a moment, sighed, and asked for a complete report of my activities in Edenberg.

I laid them out, excluding the details of my dinner with Agatha to avoid giving him unnecessary concerns. At the end he shook his head.

"A truly unsavory group of people. And instead of narrowing the field you appear to've broadened it considerably."

"That's the way it usually goes in the beginning."

"Well, it seems to me the key element in this is the undertaker. Where he was at the time of the murder and where he is now. You plan to call Minneapolis again tomorrow?"

I nodded and lit my cigarette.

He shook his head. "I never heard of an undertaker killing people before. It seems unnatural."

I let that ride and outlined my view of the whole business.

"We've got two motive choices, money and jealousy. If Maxie Hicks was murdered, I'd guess money. He was supposed to be one of the investors and probably knew who else was in and how much it amounted to. Somebody else involved didn't want him talking to me. But if Hicks died by accident, I'd figure we look for the husbands or lovers Felton crossed. Oh, I meant to ask, did Felton offer you a chance to invest in his tavern?"

Frykman considered me a moment with his sad eyes while he weighed the gall of that question against what had gone before.

"No," he said at last. "I suspect he knew it'd be futile. My reputation for conservatism is well known in Hope and Felton was too thin-skinned to relish rejection."

If that was true, I thought, he was the rarest kind of successful salesman I'd ever heard of. Most wouldn't recognize no in anything milder than physical assault.

"Who else in town has money to invest?" I asked.

"I can't think of anyone."

"Know anybody that needs money real bad?"

"Just about everybody."

That reminded me of my shortage, and we spent a while going over my expenses. I'd written them down, but he had to go over every outlay. In the end I got the impression he wasn't at all worried about being swindled, he just wanted everything spelled out. He accepted my treating Lois Simpson to lunch and didn't beef about my fancy hotel room, although he let me know it was above my station. In the end he took money from a cash box in his desk and laid it out on my palm.

I felt flush as a winning gambler.

"What're you going to do next?" he asked. "Besides call Minneapolis tomorrow?"

"I'll talk with McCoy's secretary Lois again. See if she knows anything about Maxie Hicks and maybe poke her to see how she reacts when she knows I've heard about the battle for her between her boss and his top salesman."

"All right. One more thing. I suggest it'd be wise to avoid visiting Florence Fogel again. There's no point in goading Officer Ruppman into some foolish act."

For several seconds I stared at him while he stirred, cleared his throat, and met my eyes.

"I'm sorry," he said at last. "The truth is, Officer Ruppman is not altogether rational where Florence is concerned. I realize he doesn't frighten you but as I've said before, I want to avoid embarrassment and a clash between you two would be very bad. Very."

"As bad as between Felton and Ruppman?"

He didn't finish. "I've no reason to believe there was a confrontation between those two. Florence rejected Felton's attentions. She has not rejected yours, if I understand what's going on. And in all fairness, you mustn't let your personal involvement cloud your judgment in this matter."

"I won't. But you'd better not get so worried about being embarrassed you ignore some facts. Has anybody looked at the slug from Felton's skull? Do you know it didn't come from Ruppman's .38?"

"Officer Ruppman sent the bullet to Aquatown for study. I don't know that he's had a report yet."

I settled back in my chair. "Ruppman sent it. You think about that any?"

The sadness in his eyes was enough to choke up a buzzard.

"Evidently," he said, "I'll have to. In any event, please don't provoke Ruppman. I'll pursue the question of the bullet directly with authorities in Aquatown. Meanwhile, be discreet."

I walked discreetly as I could back to the hotel. I was on the sidewalk in front when it happened.

I felt heat pass my neck before hearing the shot and hit

the pavement, expecting more. Two came before I skinned around the corner. It didn't seem wise to expect the sniper was out of range so I rabbit-ran until I got to a rain barrel and ducked behind it by the hotel's back shed.

Everything was so quiet my puffing was the loudest sound in the night.

18

Tuesday morning Frykman, Ruppman, and I went over what had happened the night before, including the search Ruppman made with me for spent slugs when he showed up in response to the shooting. I figured the shots had come from across the street, east of where I'd been walking, or from a parked car I'd spotted just south. I didn't think it'd been a Ford but wasn't sure because elms between the car and the streetlight kept it too hidden. By the time Ruppman showed up and I got around to looking, the car was gone.

Ruppman had dug the first slug out of the wall before we scrabbled around the walk looking for the others, without luck. Or at least I had none. Of course if Ruppman had been the sniper he'd know better where to look and what to hide.

He showed Frykman the slug he'd found and told him, with what seemed to me great satisfaction, that it'd hit a nail in the wall that smashed it all to hell, so there was no telling what kind of gun it came from.

"All I'm sure of is it's too heavy for a .22 and not heavy enough for any other rifle."

"Likely a .38 pistol," I said, looking at the gun on his hip.

"If it'd been me, I wouldn't've missed," he bragged.

Frykman frowned on the nasties and suggested I used

Ruppman's phone for my call to Minneapolis about the undertaker. I half expected Ruppman would object but he didn't, and in a couple minutes Logan was on the line.

"Your man never showed up," he said. "No cancellation, no show."

I thanked him and reported to Frykman. He looked at Ruppman, who moved me away from the telephone and asked the operator to ring Mrs. Clint.

She answered and he told her what we'd learned. After a moment's listening he asked for her daughter's telephone number. He scowled. "You don't have it? Your own daughter?"

He listened skeptically a few seconds longer, then asked for the address. She didn't have that either. Finally he hung up.

"She says the daughter moved last week and she doesn't have the new address or number. The girl was supposed to call and tell her but hasn't got around to it. She says that's typical of the kid."

"Maybe Les is searching Minneapolis for her," I suggested.

"Real funny," said Ruppman. "Mr. Mayor, how about you get this clown out of here. I got work to do."

Frykman nodded and we went out on the sidewalk. The wind was up, the sky had turned hazy with dust and heat, and it was dry enough to crack your tongue if you yawned too wide.

"I'm afraid you'll have to visit Minneapolis after all," he said. "I dread the expense but it's necessary."

"There's no train till tomorrow morning."

"I know. Mr. Severance at the Chevrolet dealer's will let you take a loaner. I'll handle it. I believe you intended to talk with Mrs. Simpson. Call from the hotel."

Lois Simpson answered the phone, recognized my voice when I asked for McCoy, and turned on the frost when she told me he was out of town.

I asked when he'd gone and where he was staying.

"Why do you ask?"

"Well, things have begun to heat up here. Somebody tried to murder me last night."

"Really?" She sounded skeptical but couldn't hide the interest.

"This guy took three shots at me outside Cole's Hotel. Close enough so I felt the heat of the first one. It's made me a little anxious to get this business straight, you know?"

"If it were me," she said, "I'd get out of town."

"Is that your advice?"

"Why do you want to know where Mr. McCoy is? What's he got to do with all this?"

"Lois, he told me himself he was a suspect. If he thinks so plenty others do, and the only way to stop that kind of thing is to find the facts and clear him, right?"

"That's not what you're after."

"You're right. I'm after who did it. If you think it's not McCoy, give me any help you can so I don't waste time on the wrong track."

She gave that a few seconds, sighed, and told me he was staying at the Lincoln Hotel in Aquatown, where he was meeting with some other district managers and a man from their national headquarters.

I thanked her, said she'd been a big help, and then asked if she knew Maxie Hicks. She knew about him. Everybody did. She also said word was out that his death was accidental. The fire'd been started by his own cigarette. "It was in the paper last night. The article mentioned you."

"How?"

"It said you were a private detective investigating the murder of Felton Edwards. It made you seem very mysterious."

"Great. Listen, did Felton ever talk to you about his idea for a tavern?"

"Yes. He even asked me to invest in it. When I said I didn't have money for such a thing he said I could borrow because it'd be like an investment and he could offer security. I wasn't interested."

"What'd McCoy and Felton scrap about?"

"Who says they did?"

"McCoy told me himself. It must've been pretty violent, because he said that's why people in town might think he'd done the shooting."

"That's nonsense. It was never that bad."

"I've heard they scrapped over you."

She didn't gasp or even make an immediate denial, but after a moment she said it was certainly unbelievable what things people would gossip about.

"Lois, did they both make a play for you?"

"It was nothing like that at all. Mr. McCoy's just very protective and considerate of me. He depends on me a great deal and when Fel—Mr. Edwards—took me to lunch and brought me back a few minutes late it made Mr. McCoy crazy. That made Mr. Edwards sure Mr. McCoy was, you know, romantic about me when he told him to leave me alone. That's just funny, when you think about it. But Mr. McCoy getting mad made him vulnerable in Mr. Edwards's eyes and he just had to exploit that."

"How do you mean?"

"Well, he just kept making double-meaning remarks, implying there was something going on between Mr. McCoy and me. There was something threatening about it, like he might make a scandal of it if Mr. McCoy weren't careful. . . . Does all this sound crazy?"

"No."

"Oh, I'm glad you said that. I thought you might understand. Most people'd think I was being simple or worse."

"What's worse?"

"Well, devious."

"Mrs. Simpson," I said, "you're priceless."

I asked her for other people she could name that were close to Felton, but she said she simply didn't know any.

I called the Lincoln Hotel in Aquatown, and in a few minutes had McCoy on the line. Yes, he said, he'd been there all night and had played poker with a gang of guys until after midnight. I asked if he could give me their names and he said damn right and did.

As I headed for Severance's Chevy shop I decided it wasn't likely McCoy'd shot at me. He was too easy and quick with the names. Unless, of course, they were cronies that'd lie for him. But I didn't think he'd have buddies that loyal.

▽

19

THE CAR WAS A brown Dodge about a year old, good enough but not so classy I felt like stopping in Corden to show it off when I took 212 through. At Montevideo, Minnesota, I switched to Highway 7 and wheeled through towns like Clara City, Prinsburg, and Cedar Mills. Stopped for supper in Hutchinson and walked around enough to look at the surrounding prairie, which didn't seem brown as South Dakota's. It got better as I neared Minneapolis with its lakes and trees, and turned worse when I got into town traffic and all the confusion.

Remembering Frykman's cracks about extravagant living, I picked a cheap hotel on Hennepin and, after a stroll past the movie theaters and bars, stopped for a beer in a joint that shouldn't have embarrassed the mayor and tried out the telephone in a booth by the front door. An operator with a voice soothing as a ripsaw told me Elaine Clint's telephone had been disconnected. I asked if she could give me the last address listed and she did. There, a broad, sleepy-eyed woman caretaker coyly let me know she might be able to find the forwarding address if I had a loose five handy. I came up with it.

It was about nine when I drove out Portland Avenue almost to Lake Street, parked in front of a big house, and walked slowly toward its wide screen porch. There were no lights inside, but the glare from Lake Street showed me two people watching my approach in silence.

I mounted the first step and said hi through the screen.

A man rose from a rocker and came to the door. He was tall and bent.

"I'm trying to find Elaine Clint," I said. "Is she here?"

"What's your business with her?" The voice was deep but wheezy, as if he had a leak in his windpipe.

"Her father's missing. Her mother's worried, asked me to check with Elaine, see if he's been in touch."

"She ought to worry about her daughter too, then," he said. "She moved into our room upstairs last week and we haven't seen her since she left the morning after."

When I was seated across from them on a bench with my back to the street, his missus started filling me in on what they knew. She didn't have any trouble with her breathing or talking, which came in a voice almost deep as his. She said Elaine was pretty, glib, and sweet as a sugar cookie.

"And," she added, "lied like a trooper."

"How so?"

"I asked where she worked and she said in the women's wear at Dayton's. I asked where she came from and she said a little town named Clint in South Dakota which was named after her grandfather, who started it, and where her papa was a banker. She was so wide-eyed and sweet I took it all in and believed every word, but when she went off in the morning and never came back I called Dayton's and they never heard of her. I looked up a map of South Dakota and couldn't find any town named Clint. Can you imagine a girl spinning a story like that?"

Then, after studying me in the dark, she asked what my name was, where I came from, and how come Mrs. Clint asked me to check things out. I didn't lie a lot except maybe by omission and tried to give her the notion I was a family friend with nothing better to do, but her experience with Elaine had spoiled her innocence and I could feel she wasn't buying it.

"Did she leave stuff in the room?" I asked.

"Not a hairpin. She must've packed her bag and hauled it off when she left, which was before we were up."

"You sure she spent the night?"

"Oh yes, we heard the toilet flush in the morning while we were still in bed."

"I didn't," he wheezed.

The old woman giggled. "He wouldn't. He don't wanna believe that young woman uses the toilet."

I asked if I could look at the room. After a moment's hesitation she said okay and came along with me, turning on lights as we went up. There was direct access to the room through an entry hall at the head of the stairs. The room was large, with two big windows overlooking the street. There was a navy blue overstuffed chair, a well-polished six-drawer bureau, a double bed with a light blue spread, and a deep closet. The carpet was dark blue. I looked in the closet and the bureau but as the lady said, her brief guest hadn't left a thing.

"Is that connected?" I asked, nodding at a telephone on a stand beside the bed.

"Yes. Fella that lived here before put it in and it's paid for through the month so we didn't have it cut off. Actually that was a clincher for Elaine. She was real tickled to see a phone in. I only hope she didn't run up any long-distance calls on it. Maybe you better give me her folks' address so I can get on them if she did."

I didn't know the address but made one up I figured was close and figured in a town that size, the name of the funeral home would be enough.

I asked if she remembered hearing the telephone ring and she said no, but she'd never heard it ring when Jason was there either so maybe it did and maybe it didn't.

"You tried to rent the room yet?" I asked when we were back on the porch.

"Nope," she said, and for the first time smiled. "She paid two weeks in advance."

$\triangledown$

20

THERE WAS LITTLE POINT in calling detectives Logan and Flynn the next morning, since none of the dope offered by Elaine's landlords would be any help. After I'd stewed over my alternatives, the best route seemed to be going into disguise.

So I drifted around to a Salvation Army store, rummaged through stacks of clothes, and came up with a suit and tie that were some shy of spiffy but might get me a shot at talking with an undertaker. The Army couldn't come up with a shirt that had enough collar for my neck without sleeves half a yard too long and I had to pop for a new one, which cost over two bucks at Penney's.

The tie gave me some trouble before I finally got a knot that would do and set off, feeling like a clown in costume.

The Radisson's doorman gave me the fishy eye but let me by with a look that suggested he was being overtolerant. Inside I located the bulletin board listing goings-on and found the undertakers' convention. The desk clerk wasn't too snooty to give me directions and even came up with the name of the outfit's president, Calvin Sherer.

It took some hanging around before there was a break in their meetings and I managed to buttonhole an important-

looking dude and explain I needed somebody to point out
Leslie Clint so I could tell him he had to call home because
of family trouble. The dude took in my outfit without laugh-
ing and referred me to a young guy who was passing. This
one was interested right away, because he said Mr. Sherer
had been asking about Clint.

A couple minutes later I was in a corner with Sherer. He
looked more like an Irish politician than an undertaker,
being well-fed, red-cheeked, and twinkly blue-eyed. He had
a good head of skin and when he grinned, which came easy,
his eyes about closed. Evidently the fact that they weren't
going to bury anybody on this jaunt had turned him sporty
and he had abandoned the black suit of his office for a gray
plaid a used car salesman would love.

I told him what I knew and how bad it looked for Clint
with his wife's boyfriend murdered and him missing. The
news flabbergasted him. He hadn't heard of the murder and
had trouble taking that in.

"Did you know about Felton and Pauline?" I asked.

"Yes, most of it. Les confides in me, we're very close. Have
been since we first met some eight years ago. I'll tell you, I've
been worried about him. It's not like Les to make a reservation, pay in advance, and not show up. He even agreed to
make a special presentation. Maybe he got stage fright—he'd
never done one for us before—"

"He was supposed to look up his daughter while in town
too, but she moved to a new place last week and after one
night hasn't been back to it."

"That's bad," he told me. "He's just crazy about Elaine.
There's all kinds of trouble in that family, you know. Bad
feelings between the mother and daughter. Mother resents
the young one's looks and youth. That's why she—the
mother—has got involved with another man. It's a mess—
but one thing I can tell you for sure, Les'd never kill anybody.
That's just totally out of character."

"Did he ever tell you anything that'd give you an idea

where he'd go if he decided he was fed up with his marriage?"

He shook his head. "He admitted to me once it might be a good idea for Polly and him to split up a while. Give her a chance to breathe is the way he put it. I think he really believed if she had a chance to see what sort of fellow she was getting herself involved with, she'd soon come back to the old reliable. Les understood Felton too—and honestly liked him. Les is always impressed by those fellows that never get enough of anything but are so fired up you can't hate them."

I could, easy. He sensed that at once and grinned.

"Okay, I should say Les couldn't. He envied people with old Felton's, God, what would you call it, hunger?"

"Greed'll do."

He laughed and said I was probably right but pretty puritanical. That notion about choked me. Ma and Pa, who are total puritans, would've fainted at the idea anybody'd think their heathen son shared their beliefs.

I asked if there was anybody else in his organization that knew Clint well, and he insisted none did as well as him.

"You know the daughter at all?"

"Met her last year, yeah. A real peach."

"Know anything about her? Any close friends, a guy?"

He considered that some and nodded. "It's not anybody I've met or anything—but Les did say there was a fella she knew at school she was set on. Had a funny name. Rolf, I think. Rolf Roddenbakker. That was it. Les didn't much like him but I don't think Les'd liked anybody his little girl got interested in."

"Why'd he say he didn't like him?"

"Oh, he was an athlete, a boxer on the school team. Les didn't think he was a serious enough man for his girl."

I found Roddenbakker in the telephone book and gave him a call but there was no answer. After lunch at a counter joint I called again with the same result and decided to drive around and look over the neighborhood. It was right near the campus a ways off Washington Avenue. I parked on the street and went up to the front door, which opened easy. Inside were mailboxes and I found one for Roddenbakker and an apartment number. So up the stairs I went and down a hall to 24, which was just beyond the floor's bathroom. My knock got nothing directly, but after the second try a door opened behind me and a little guy with a small face and big glasses told me Rolf was gone.

"You mean out, or gone?"

"All out, total gone. Left last week."

"Where?"

"Heaven."

"You mean he's dead?"

"Hell no. Went to live with his sweetie."

"So where's his sweetie live?"

"Damfiknow but wherever she is, it's gotta be heaven. You never saw a more gorgeous angel."

"He friends with anybody else in this place?"

"Sure. His buddy's right above."

I thanked him, climbed the stairs, and knocked on 34. There was movement inside, then steps, and the door opened. I looked up at a dude about six feet tall with shoulders that damned near filled the doorway.

He listened to my story about trying to find Elaine for her worried mother because of the father's disappearance and the death of a common friend. I didn't mention murder yet. When I stopped he folded thick arms and leaned against the door sill.

"That's a great yarn," he said grinning. "So you're a private eye her old lady hired to snoop around?"

"That's close. I hear your friend Rolf moved out of his place downstairs. You know where I can reach him?"

"Sure."

"Where?"

"What's it worth to you?"

"Look, chum, I'm not playing games. The girl's father's missing and the guy who was romancing her mother was shot in the face, which not only ruined his looks but killed him. Now who do you think looks good as the killer if he doesn't show up pretty damn sudden?"

The smug look left his face and he scowled. "You're telling me somebody shot Felton?"

"You're real warm."

"Jesus Christ," he said. The tone wasn't blasphemous.

"The daughter's missing too. Rented a room in town, paid two weeks in advance, left the first morning after, and hasn't been seen since. Your buddy's missing. It all gets a funny smell, right?"

He unfolded his arms, stepped back, and closed the door in my face.

I banged on the door. Nothing happened. I banged again and when it burst open I jumped back. He was way too big for slugging or shifty tricks so I half-turned and kicked him in the jaw with my heel. It worked like a sap to the back of the head, except instead of just folding he sailed into his room and hit the floor with a crash that shook the building. I followed him in, closed the door behind me, and checked him over. His jaw was only red so far and I could feel a lump starting to rise on the back of his skull but didn't think anything was broken. His breathing wasn't bad. I looked around, saw I was in a square kitchen, and got up to find a pillow in the next room, which was a study and bedroom in one. I got the pillow under his head and, when he moaned, lifted his head some and offered him water. He took it like a lamb.

He was too dazed to get mad before I started talking and in a while he sat up, shook his head, felt his jaw and skull, and muttered some, but didn't show any signs of planning combat.

Pretty soon he just sat, staring at me, until I asked if he had anything to drink and he said there was beer in the refrigerator. I got us each one, opened them, and when he was on his feet we moved into the other room and he sank into an easy chair while I sat on the edge of the bed and we both swigged from the bottles.

"You've got to be the toughest little son of a bitch I've ever met," he told me. "I feel like I got run over by a dump truck."

"Don't call me little."

"All right. I sure's hell don't want to make you mad."

We grinned at each other.

"Who the hell are you, really?" he asked. "You're not a cop, I'm damned sure."

I pretty much leveled with him. So he told me about his friends, Rolf and Elaine. He and Rolf came from a small town in Wisconsin, just across the Mississippi, had played football together on their high school team, and were into boxing at the U.

"Rolf met Elaine in an English class their freshman year and they've been steady ever since. Her parents didn't approve, think she's too young and he's a jock. They want a guy who'll take over their damned undertaking parlor. Rolf isn't interested."

"How much does Rolf know about this Felton guy?"

"Well," he said cheerfully, "he knows the guy's been cozy with her ma."

"You ever hear he made moves on Elaine?"

He took a deep breath, started to lean his head back, and thought better of it. "Yeah, I know he did. Elaine says she was kind of stuck on him when she was a kid but since she met Rolf it's been nothing doing."

"Did the mother know something was going on between her boyfriend and Elaine?"

"Nah."

I didn't see how he could be so sure but he insisted Elaine had been very careful about that.

"So are Rolf and Elaine together now?"

"Yeah."

"Can I have their address?"

"You just going to talk with them?"

"That's all."

"Okay. I'll take you over."

21

He WAS SUCH A decent guy I was sorry I'd kicked him in the jaw, and the sight of the lump on his noggin made me wince as he led me down the stairs.

"Where'd you learn that kick?" he asked as we waited out a passing streetcar at the corner.

"A cowboy novel called *Happy Hawkins*. The hero learned it from a French sailor and said he wasted the year after this guy knocked him cold looking for him. The first six months he planned to shoot him, the second he wanted to thank him because he'd learned to use it."

"I'd think you'd kill a man with less jaw than I've got."

"Not so far."

"How old're you?"

"It depends on how much I've been drinking."

He grinned. "I bet you haven't had anything today but that beer."

"This's usually my younger hour. How far we going?"

"One more block."

As we approached a small white house with a sharply peaked roof I looked up at the second-story window and briefly sighted a dream-woman's face, which quickly withdrew. As we went up the stoop I asked for his name.

"George. What's yours?"

I told him and he led me inside and up a straight flight of narrow steps. There was no landing, just a door that needed paint. George rapped on it.

It opened at once and a guy who was nearly George's twin looked down at us. His hair was light and clipped short, the eyes blue under dark, bushy brows.

"What the hell hit you?" he asked George.

"I tripped over Carl's heel. This is Carl Wilcox. I think you better talk with him."

Rolf backed up, letting us into a small kitchen with walls that met the sloping roof about four feet up. The dream-faced woman sat at a table covered with a gold cloth near the south wall and raised slender hands to shove light brown hair behind her ears. It immediately fell back around her face. The eyes were wider than her mother's and a deep blue. I realized I'd never known what color Polly's were, they'd been so hidden.

"You don't take after your mother," I said.

"I hope not—do you know her?"

"Met her a couple days ago."

She glanced at George.

"He says somebody killed Felton and your dad's missing," he told her.

The blue eyes switched back to me. "Dad's not here."

"You knew Felton was murdered?"

"A friend called to tell me, yes."

"When?"

"I think it was the morning after."

"Where'd this friend reach you?"

"Here."

"The day after you rented a place on the Southside?"

She looked frightened. "How'd you know about that?"

"I talked to the owners. They're still holding the room for you. They're worried."

"Why worry?" asked Rolf, scowling. "They got their dough."

"Some people worry about more than dough," I told him. I looked at Elaine. "You know where your dad is?"

She shook her head quickly.

"You know if he came to Minneapolis at all?"

"Is that important?"

"He sure's hell could use an alibi. Being in Minneapolis last Wednesday night'd be a dandy."

"Oh, well, then it's all right. He called me that night."

"Where from?"

"Minneapolis."

"Where in Minneapolis?"

"I didn't ask. He just wanted to tell me he was tied up and wouldn't be able to see me for a couple days—"

"How'd you know he wasn't calling from Edenberg?"

"Because when he calls long-distance it's always person-to-person and an operator's involved. There was no operator on this call."

She was proud she'd thought of that.

"Where'd you receive his call?"

"Well, let's see—"

"It was right here," said Rolf.

"How'd he know you'd be here?"

"He called me first," said George. "I passed on the number."

They all looked at me and smiled.

"Neat," I said. "Did he happen to explain to you during this conversation how come he got a reservation and made a down payment on a room at the Radisson and didn't use it?"

"No, he didn't mention that. He was upset and I think maybe he just didn't want to be with people. As a matter of fact he mentioned he might just go fishing. That's probably what he's doing."

"Where'd he go for that?"

"Probably up north at one of the lakes around Brainerd. There's Gull Lake and Horseshoe and some others he's used."

I stared at her for a while and the three of them stared back.

"Okay," I said. "You've fixed up a dandy act. But think about it a little, okay? The cops won't question you all together and they won't be impressed by how good-looking you are and what loyal stooges you've got. The easiest thing for them to do in a case like this is decide your dad's the killer and go after him. It's a nice simple case. Jealousy, the wronged husband, all that stuff. The quicker he's found, the better. They're still gonna suspect him, but it won't be a foregone conclusion."

Elaine started to cry, and both guys glared at me.

"He didn't really call at all, did he?"

She shook her head and cried louder.

"Leave her alone," said Rolf. "Just get the hell out of here."

"She's not helping her dad by lying. I don't blame her for trying but it's no good. The best thing she can do is help find him and let me talk with him. If he didn't do it, chances are he can prove it. If he did, he might get off easy. Juries don't go soggy over guys like Felton Edwards."

Elaine kept crying and Rolf yelled at me, telling me to get the hell out.

"I'm right," I told George. "You know it, don't you?"

He nodded and eased between Rolf and me. "We'll go," he told his friend. "Don't get excited, okay? I'll call you."

"Just get him out," yelled Rolf.

I looked at Elaine and started for the stairs but before we were halfway down she was at the door calling me back.

We went up and she asked me to sit down and told the two guys to leave us alone. Rolf objected, getting louder than ever, and she stared at him with a look that choked him off. He tried to talk calmly while she kept staring at him, with her eyes suddenly as narrow as her mother's. When he shut up she said again they should leave us alone. Rolf gave his pal George a despairing look and started down the steps. George followed, closing the door behind him.

Elaine mopped her eyes with a dish towel and sat across

from me. It took a few minutes for her to pull together but finally, with her elbows on the table and her hands folded like a little girl in class, she told me she'd called home as soon as she settled into her new room, probably about five-thirty, and talked with her father. She wanted to tell him she'd moved so he'd find her when he came, and the next thing she knew they were talking about Felton. Her father had, at first, been explaining that he'd wanted to bring her mother on this trip and Polly had absolutely refused. When he'd accused her of wanting to be alone with her lover, she'd admitted it.

"I couldn't believe it was Daddy telling me all this," Elaine said. "He's always been so private and reserved, so in control and above everything—" She choked up and took a few seconds to get her voice back. "I got mad and told him Mother wasn't good enough for him and totally lost my mind when he said it was probably his fault, he'd let himself get fat and thoughtless. It was then I told him Felton had tried to make me when I was only fourteen and that he'd called me just a few days before I moved, which was why I moved, so he couldn't find me."

She started to cry again. I sat looking from the top of her head to the street beyond the window beside me and back. Finally I reached over and put my hands on her elbows. After a moment she drew away, got up, found the dish towel again, excused herself, and went off to the bathroom.

I looked down at the street and saw Rolf and George slowly walking the sidewalk on the other side. Rolf was talking and they didn't look up.

Elaine came back, white and drained. She sat, leaned back, and met my eyes.

"Would you believe? When I was fourteen I loved that bastard. Total freshman little girl crush. He picked me up from school one afternoon, took me for a ride, and tried to do it to me, but he was so big I was terrified and got hysterical and he didn't force me. He said I embarrassed him. Really. Made me actually feel guilty! Can you imagine? My God!"

She looked across the street and shook her head. "If Rolf knew, he'd kill him. George'd help."

"But they don't know?"

She shook her head violently. "No one knows but Daddy."

Her eyes came back to me and leaned forward. "You're not a policeman, are you? I got that straight, didn't I?"

"I'm just an unofficial handyman for the mayor of Hope, trying to figure out who killed Felton. I don't have a badge or any job other than that."

"Why does anybody care who killed him?"

"Well, murder's not much accepted even when it seems the right thing to do now and then. Guys like Hope's mayor get nervous about stuff like that."

"You don't think they'd believe me if I say I was talking to Daddy in Minneapolis that night?"

"I can't say. But think a long time before you let those two friends of yours get in trouble lying for you."

"I won't have Daddy go to prison because of that bastard Felton and my bitch mother!"

"You think he did it, don't you?"

"Oh God!" she cried. "I don't know. He sure had reasons, didn't he?"

"Yeah. Did he own a gun?"

At first I didn't think she was going to answer but finally she slumped forward, folding her arms across her breast and lowering her head.

"It's bound to come out, isn't it? Everything'll come out. Yes. He had a gun. A pistol. My uncle gave it to him a long time ago. I don't think Daddy ever fired it in his life."

"Where's your uncle?"

"He died a long time ago. When I was twelve or so."

"Okay. Where do you think your dad is?"

"I don't know!" she wailed. "He had no place to go, nobody to care but me . . ."

That was all I could get from her, and in the end it seemed likely that's all she had.

22

I TELEPHONED LOGAN, the Minneapolis cop, late in the afternoon and went over everything.

"It's gotta be the undertaker, Clint," he said. "He's got the motive in spades, owned the gun. The way I see it, this was a sudden mad-on killing. The talk with the kid—what's her name? Elaine? That tripped it. The guy screwing his wife didn't get to him so much but when he not only screwed her but kept her from traveling with him to see their daughter and on top of that had tried to lay the kid too—hell, that'd even make an undertaker kill. Especially when he had a gun handy. Nothing like a temper and a gun for adding up to murder. Now he's probably drinking himself stiff and'll wind up either eating his gun or turning himself in, crazy with guilt and wanting to confess. His kind do it every time."

I saw it pretty much the same way and said I'd try to get a picture of the man so they could circulate it in case Clint was holing up in Minneapolis.

It was after midnight when I got back to the Cole Hotel in Hope, and it was ten and getting hot when I woke starkers on the thin sheet.

By ten-thirty Mary was cheerfully taking my pancakes and

bacon order, and before eleven she came around to tell me
Mayor Frykman wanted me in his office.

My report made his sad eyes get an almost cheerful glow
as he became convinced the killer wasn't from Hope. He said
Severance had reported I'd returned the rented car in good
condition, which suggested that neither of them had held
high hopes in that regard.

I told him Logan wanted a picture of Clint for circulation
around Minneapolis, and suggested Ruppman would be the
proper guy to ask the Edenberg police to get it. At the same
time he could let them know the man was wanted for questioning in a murder case. Frykman promised he'd take care
of it.

It was near noon by then and I decided it was too soon for
lunch, got into my Model T, and headed to the west side,
where I'd left off painting.

After lunch I called Clint's wife to ask about survivors of
her husband's brother. She turned snotty and said she wasn't
answering any questions until I told her everything I'd
learned in Minneapolis about her daughter, Elaine. I said I'd
talked with her but omitted a few choice details, like the fact
she was living with her boyfriend and despised her mother.

"What'd you find out about my husband?"

"Nothing you don't know—except that he owned a gun.
A little detail you skipped telling about."

"Elaine told you that?"

"Uh-huh."

It was plain that surprised her, but she made no comment
and suddenly answered my earlier question. She said the
only surviving relatives of Leslie's brother were Les and his
family.

"Where's your son?" I asked.

"He works on a weekly newspaper in a small town near
Columbia, Missouri. As I told you, he's an outstanding
student—that's why he was offered this job. Like an appren-
ticeship. If you think his father's with him, forget it. They
aren't close."

"That's why he didn't come home for the summer?"

She admitted as much.

I asked for the name of the town where he was working and after some hesitation she told me. Then she tried pumping me some more, but finally realized she was working a dry well and hung up.

Mac McGillacuddy showed around two or so, this time pedaling slow and easy up the hill.

"No new bodies?" I said.

He shook his red head and stood straddling the crossbar.

I put my brush down and rolled a cigarette. He paid such close attention I couldn't resist showing off and doing it single-handed. His eyes bugged.

"You smoke?" I asked.

"Tried it," he confessed.

"Didn't like it?"

He shook his head. "Made me cough. My aunt said it made me stink."

"She's right. Think you could learn to paint signs?"

"Nah. Can't hardly write so you can read it. But one day I'll get one of those typewriters and it won't matter."

Since I didn't need an apprentice there was no point in pushing him, so I asked if he'd ever thought how come that tall galoot got himself killed in a sandpit in a town he hadn't visited in near fifteen years.

He shrugged. I asked if he talked to his aunt about it and he nodded. She told him somebody probably brought him there to do it or maybe did it somewhere else and thought the sandpit a good place to leave the body.

"When'd that guy come around to see your aunt?"

"When I was real little."

"That's why he looked familiar, right? You'd seen him with your aunt?"

He put the bike on the ground, sat beside it and squinted at me. "Yeah."

"Were they pretty friendly?"

He shrugged.

"Did he touch her?"

"No."

"They just talked."

He nodded.

I tried to get more but when he avoided my questions and my eyes I knocked it off, butted out my cigarette, and started painting.

"You gonna come to our house again?" he asked after a while.

"You want me to?"

He allowed he wouldn't mind.

"How about your aunt, would she mind?"

He didn't think so. "She likes giving people tea."

I figured that probably got him cookies but decided there could be more on his mind.

"Does Ruppman come around a lot?" I asked.

"Uh-huh. Sometimes in his car and sometimes walking by."

"Keeps an eye on things, huh?"

He nodded again.

I asked if Ruppman ever talked to him and he said he had now and then. Mostly he wanted to know who visited.

"I'm supposed to tell him when guys come around," he said.

"Why's that?" I asked.

"He's gotta pertect her. Some guys aren't nice."

"So when I come around you tell him, right?"

"I don't have to."

"Does your aunt know he told you to let him know about guys?"

"He told me not to tell her but I did. I tell her everything."

"And she tells you?"

"Uh-huh."

"That's good."

As far as he was concerned it was natural. I guessed that would last until he found girls more important than Florence.

Finally he got to his feet, straddled the bike, and walked it around until he was facing downtown.

"My aunt says if you want, you can have supper at our place tonight."

I thanked him and said I'd be around. And then I wondered how come it'd taken him so long to deliver that invitation, which must've been on his mind all the time we talked.

And what was Florence up to? She sure as hell knew I'd been shot at the last time I'd visited her and probably had as good an idea as I who'd done it. So was she positive it was nothing but Ruppman trying to scare me, or did she want to settle something?

Well, I'd find out.

▽

23

IT WAS NEAR FIVE when I got back to the hotel and Cole asked about my Minneapolis trip. Knowing he'd stretch anything he heard and broadcast it before dark, I kept my story short.

He dug hard for details on the missing undertaker and was unhappy I wouldn't say flat out he was the killer, but no doubt he'd work out the details to suit himself for the first listener he found.

I asked if the flashy redhead was still with us.

"You mean Mrs. Amberly?"

"How many redheaded women you got staying here?"

"She's the onliest one," he admitted, grinning evilly. "She says you got fresh with her last week. I told her she oughtn't take it serious, you didn't mean nothing by it."

"How'd you know that?"

"I didn't," he giggled. "Just wanted to ease her mind. You gonna go see Florence tonight?"

"Cole, you gotta be the nosiest bastard I've met."

"Probably. Everybody's waiting to see what Ruppman'll do if you try. Some bet you will, some go the other way."

"What's your bet?"

"You'll go."

"Don't bet the hotel on it."

While he laughed I asked where the redhead came from.

"Fargo."

That threw me. She looked like at least Minneapolis, maybe even Chicago.

"What's she doing here?"

"I asked but all she said was it was 'personal.' Nobody could say 'none of your business' nicer than that, huh?"

"When'd she get here?"

He grinned. "The night Felton Edwards got shot."

He said that like he figured it was something to make me think, but just then I was more involved with my visit to Flo's house. The approaches came down to driving over, taking a hike and coming down from the west to her back door, or simply walking straight from the hotel. It seemed that driving straight would reduce the exposure. Obviously, coming back to the hotel would be the danger time.

I drove over. Ruppman was nowhere in sight along the way but that was no comfort since I hadn't seen him the time before either.

By five Florence's little house threw a shadow almost to the street and the shade felt good as I approached the front porch. Mac and Florence were both at the door by the time I reached the stoop and it almost seemed as though they'd been waiting there since my last visit. Her hair glowed gold through the screen and when she let me in her hazel eyes, rosy face, and warm smile hit me as the prettiest sight in South Dakota.

"Well," she said, "you came."

"Ma always told me, never pass up an invitation to supper."

"And you've always done exactly what your mother told you to?"

"Only when she was right."

We went into her little living room, which was dark and cozy, with the drapes still closed against the hot sun of morning and early afternoon. She left me with Mac to go do something in the kitchen and he asked how it felt to get shot at. I told him it wasn't a lot of fun.

"Was it Ruppman?" he asked.

"I don't know—do you?"

"Everybody says it was."

"You think they're right?"

He looked troubled. "He never shot any of the other guys. Hit one with his fist, though."

We both thought that over some and then he said, "Mr. Ruppman doesn't like me."

"Why'd you think that?"

"The way he talks to me."

"Like at the sandpit?"

He nodded.

"That didn't mean anything. He was shook up, seeing the body and figuring all the headaches it'd give him."

Mac wasn't impressed.

We went directly from the living room into the kitchen when Florence called us to supper. There was no dining room. The square kitchen table stood against the west wall by a window through which I could see the small gray outhouse at the far southwest corner of the lot. Grapevines climbed a trellis on its south side and there was the usual quarter-moon hole cut above the door.

We ate fried chicken, sweet potatoes done in a casserole under marshmallows toasted golden brown, fresh green peas, and baking-powder biscuits with homemade grape jelly. Between us Mac and I polished off the dark meat, while Florence hardly wounded the breast.

There was devil's food cake with fudge frosting for dessert, and while dutifully working on it I decided if this was my last meal I couldn't have ordered better.

I asked how much she'd seen of Felton and she said very little. When she was still in her teens she'd worked a year as a maid and eventually cook for a widow who was well off in money but poor in health. The old lady died and left a small amount to Florence, who spent the windfall on her trip to

Minneapolis, where she went to the university for a year and a half. Felton had come to the house of the widow when Florence worked there, at first trying to persuade the old lady to buy insurance. He came back pretending to be just friendly but made a strong pitch at Florence, who said she gave him no encouragement.

"It might've been different if I hadn't had a crush on Johnnie Powers. Felton was all charm and good humor and had a way about him that seemed sincere to me back then. I enjoyed his attention but thought it was just funny when he told me what a beauty and heartbreaker I was. When I came back from Minneapolis with Mac, Felton popped up again. It wasn't at all pleasant that time. Awful, in fact. He was convinced I was a loose woman and came on too strong. I told him where he could go. He showed up again about two years ago, being cute, and we had some laughs but he got nowhere. I finally set him down hard and he never came back, which was fine with me."

"Was Johnnie Powers surprised when you showed up at the U?"

"No. We'd talked about it when we were seeing each other in senior high. He was all excited when I first got to Minneapolis and we were together a lot for a couple months but then he got involved with his fraternity and all the fellows there were going with sorority girls who came from families with money and wore great clothes and all that. I couldn't compete. And then the second year I was in school my sister and her husband died in a car accident, leaving Mac alone, so I got him and came back to Hope."

She washed the dishes after supper and I helped Mac dry them. When he took off on his bike we sat in the living room with coffee.

"You surprised me," she said as she put her cup down.

"Because I didn't eat my peas with a knife?"

She laughed. "No. It was your helping with the dishes. I expected you'd just smoke and watch us clean up."

"When a meal's that good, I feel I owe something."

"There's no flavoring to beat a good appetite, but thank you. I wanted you to enjoy it. Mac likes you."

"How come he took off?"

"I told him to. Before you came. He'll be back before dark."

"That doesn't give us much time."

"That was the idea."

We kissed pretty much like the last time but she cut me off at the pass when I checked to see if I could move inside the dress or stretch her out on the couch. As long as we sat fairly straight and just smooched she was easy to get along with and warm as I'd like.

Finally she gave me a really good pressure kiss, pushed me away, and stood.

"Mac'll be back any minute. You want more coffee?"

I said okay, she brought it, turned on a lamp, fluffed her hair a touch, and sat primly in a chair out of reach.

"Maybe you should leave before it gets really dark," she said.

"You think Ruppman'll take another crack at me?"

"No. I warned him if anything happened to you I'd leave Hope."

"When'd you tell him that?"

"When he was here this afternoon. We had a rather straightforward conversation."

"Did he admit shooting at me?"

"No. He denied it. I said it didn't matter whether it was him or someone else, if you got hurt I'd leave. He told me quite a bit about you. He says you've a scandalous reputation with women and your wife divorced you for faithlessness and that you've been in prison several times."

"Only twice."

She smiled. "Was that the only inaccuracy?"

"It was the clearest."

"Why'd you go to prison?"

"Mainly because they didn't offer any choice. You see, the first time I needed money to help a lady with a kid and no job or husband. I got snockered and tried holding up a jewelry store with an empty gun. The jeweler was no trouble, but this old woman customer wouldn't get on the floor—just put her hands up. A passing cop caught the scene and charged in waving his cannon and I put my gun on the counter and claimed it was all a practical joke. The judge wasn't convinced and while sentencing me asked if I had any regrets. I said yeah, I was sorry I hadn't made the lady get on the floor."

Florence didn't look too horrified so I told her about working for the widow in Montana who didn't have enough cattle so I went off to borrow some. On the getaway my horse stepped in a gopher hole and broke his leg.

"You seem to have been a sadly inept Robin Hood."

That was a kind way to put it. Before I could thank her, Mac showed up. It gave me one clue as to why he might've been right when he thought Ruppman didn't like him.

I drove back to the hotel keeping an eye out for parked cars and snipers but saw nothing suspicious and got home unshot.

Ruppman was sitting in the deserted lobby when I entered.

▽

24

"You taking over for Cole?" I asked.

"Never mind the smartass line. I didn't ask for your help, don't want it, but since the mayor's hired you he might's well get his money's worth. What've you found out?"

I told him most of it and summed up with a list of my favorite suspects, which ended with him.

He snorted. "You spent three days running all over the state and came up with sniffles."

"And what've you got, sitting here?"

"I know he was killed with a .38 and it wasn't mine. And I got a report from the coroner in Edenberg, who says the Hicks guy died of smoke. They're not sure about arson."

"You find Felton's car?"

"Don't even know what he was driving. There's no unaccounted-for cars in Hope. I've talked with the chief in Edenberg and they're checking around. If it's in a private garage, God knows when we'll find it."

"According to a witness in Edenberg, he was driving a Packard there last week."

"Jeez—thanks for telling me—"

"So somebody drove him there or they went in his car and the killer drove it out. Anybody seen Les Clint's car?"

"Uh-huh. It's sitting in his garage where he left it. Pauline says he never drove to the cities, hated long drives and city traffic. Says he got a ride with an undertaker friend from Doland last year, but when I called the friend he said he couldn't go this year and hadn't a notion who Clint might've found to ride with."

"And Polly didn't see him picked up?"

"You got it. She says she was up in her room when he left. Didn't even hear him go out. The hired girl and the yardman had the evening off."

"Handy. Did Polly tell you she and Les had a scrap before he left?"

"Yeah, she admitted that. He wanted her to go along and she wouldn't. Said a gang of undertakers bored her stiff. He got in a snit, packed his bag, went downstairs, and that's the last she saw of him."

We sat quietly for a few seconds.

"We've got to find out where the hell Felton was during the six months after he quit McCoy," I said. "McCoy's secretary says he left a general delivery address in Aquatown. How about I call Lieutenant Baker there and see if he can dig up something?"

"Baker's a buddy of yours?"

"We've met."

"I'll bet."

He got up, walked to the door, and paused for a moment, scowling at me.

"Okay. Come over to my office in the morning and call him."

He started to push out the screen, stopped, and gave me a mean look. "One other thing, Wilcox. You give Florence any grief, any at all, and I'll get you. Don't ever forget it."

"I'll try to keep it in mind."

He glared a moment, then went out and closed the door carefully behind him.

I heard him speak to someone as I headed for the stairs and paused to glance back when the door opened and the tony redhead stepped into the lobby, followed by a slick-haired, potbellied man about my height. This, I guessed, was Eric Atwater, Attorney at Law. I turned and drifted back into the lobby as Cole appeared in the cubbyhole behind the check-in counter and beamed at everybody.

Cole made introductions. For the first time the redheaded woman met my eyes. Hers were so green they looked fake. Her name was Felicia Amberly. I was right about the man; he was the lawyer she'd visited a few days earlier. After introductions she excused herself and went upstairs. Eric Atwater sat in a rocker and studied me with judging eyes.

"I know Howie Granger," he said. "He's spoken of you quite a lot."

No good response came to mind, since anything he'd heard from Howie wasn't likely to be flattering. Howie was the young lawyer who helped my old bachelor buddy, Boswell, in one case for me, and my widowed client, Trixie, in another.

"As you may have guessed," said the lawyer, "I'm representing Mrs. Amberly. Her uncle, Lyman Amberly, died a month ago. He was quite well off, very old, and slightly senile before his passing. It seems he saw a great deal of the man who was murdered, Felton Edwards, during his final days, and may have turned over a substantial amount of money to Edwards for some sort of scheme he'd been led to believe was a safe investment."

"In Aquatown?"

His eyebrows lifted. "Yes, as a matter of fact—how'd you know?"

"It was easy."

"Yes, well, I've been making inquiries and have had no luck locating any heirs for Mr. Edwards. I haven't even been able to find a last address for him. I wondered if you might have come up with anything?"

"You talked with Ruppman?"

"He knows nothing."

"Why'd you think I might?"

"It's easy, I know you're working for our mayor and I'm confident it's not simply as a sign painter."

"I don't have an address either. If the old man was senile, did he have a caretaker?"

"Yes. A private nurse. I tried to talk with her. She took offense when I let slip my suspicions that Edwards was a con man. Evidently she admired him excessively, because she immediately took umbrage and was totally uncooperative. I thought perhaps you could approach her more effectively."

"What's it worth?"

"A daily expense account and a bonus if you can locate the money my client's uncle turned over to him. I understand the corpse was searched and the pockets stripped?"

"He didn't even have lint left."

"Yes, well, I think it unlikely he was carrying several thousand dollars on his person, don't you?"

"Why'd you think he'd have that kind of money?"

"Because I understand there's a check missing from Mr. Amberly's book. My client thinks Felton stole it and committed forgery. This hasn't been confirmed as yet."

I shrugged and got him down to my pay. He was easy to deal with, so I knew it wouldn't come out of his pocket.

As he got up to leave I asked if Felicia Amberly was a widow. He smiled.

"Her husband died two years ago, come November. He was considerably her senior. She writes things, used to be an actress, sang in amateur musicals. A very modern woman. And very handsome, don't you think?"

"What's she do with her time here?"

"She observes. Writes. She's working on an article about life in small towns during the Depression. Can't imagine who'd buy it, but it amuses her and she's not pressed for money."

"How come she didn't choose Aquatown, where she could get a better hotel?"

"I was puzzled by that myself. When I asked, she said she was more interested in the truly small communities and felt

a trifle wary about Aquatown. She told me she might work
up to that after studying the villages nearby first. I think
she's a romantic."

He really figured her for a bubblehead.

We shook hands before he left. For a lawyer he had a good
grip.

Next morning, as I was parking my hinder on a stool at
the counter in Winkle's Café, Mary told me the lady in the
booth wanted me to join her. I glanced in the mirror, saw the
redhead looking my way, and went over.

She studied my face as I sat across from her. Nothing in
her expression gave a hint of what she thought she saw.

"Eric told me some things about you," she said. "He's also
admitted leaving out a great deal. I have a vague impression
you're something of a renegade."

"That's not far off."

"Interesting. I understand there's a tradition in the West
of hiring former gunmen as lawmen. That strikes me as
something like appointing a wolf to guard the sheep."

"The trick's to make him find it's better guarding them
than eating them."

"Are you a drinker?"

"Now and again."

"Yes, I imagine so. And you've been a cowboy, hobo, and
soldier?"

"And a cop."

"I understand you're going to Aquatown to check into Mr.
Edwards's activities there."

"Yeah. This weekend."

"I've talked with Mayor Frykman. He's willing for you to
go today. I want to travel with you."

"You won't like my car."

"We can take the one you used to visit Minneapolis. I've
rented it."

Mary delivered my breakfast and I started in on it.

"Well," said the redhead, "you haven't agreed to take me."

"What's to agree? You got everything lined up. Fine."

"You're not surprised?"

"I'm impressed."

She nodded. I wished she'd smile.

"You aren't really from Fargo, are you?" I said.

"No. Philadelphia. I registered from Fargo because people here don't trust easterners. I have a cousin who lives in Fargo and was visiting her this spring. She'd been here in Hope for a time, visiting an old aunt of hers, and told me enough about this little town to make me feel it'd be a good one to write about."

She talked casually, asking for my impressions of townspeople, and never smiled or laughed. Usually I find only guys can be humorless, and I've never been able to stand that kind. Meeting a woman who was good-looking and smart but never laughed threw me. There had to be something she found funny, but I couldn't find it.

She asked how long it'd take to drive to Aquatown. I said about an hour or so.

"All right. Let's leave in half an hour. The car's gassed up and ready."

I was still drinking my coffee when she left, and when I went up to pay for my breakfast Mary told me with cold disapproval it'd already been covered.

▽

25

Felicia spent the trip asking questions about the pains and pleasures of running a small-town hotel, the attitudes of small-towners toward farmers and vice versa, and details of my family. Her eyes got wide when I told her Ma claimed she'd walked beside a covered wagon from New York State to the Dakotas.

"Why'd she have to walk?"

"I'm not sure. Of course Ma always was hefty—maybe it was to ease things for the oxen."

She frowned. "That's hard to believe."

"Yeah, I never swallowed it myself, since Ma claims she was only four at the time. It seemed a bit much for a toddler."

She gave me a long sober look and changed the subject to my two hitches in the army and the months I spent beach-combing in the Philippines after I was kicked out of service the last time for errors in judgment, like punching out a first sergeant.

Her uncle's place in Aquatown stood on a corner lot in a block loaded with minor mansions, set well back on lawns big enough to graze cattle and kept green with regular watering. The three-story house had a whopping screened porch across the front and around both sides. The south wall was shaded by giant oaks and there were hedges edging the entire porch. Nobody answered my knock but I noticed a curtain move in a house to the north and suggested we check over there. A young girl answered the chimes a moment after I poked the button on the front door. She was blue-eyed, blond, and pretty enough to put on a Christmas tree. I introduced my partner as her former neighbor's niece and asked if she or anyone else in the house could tell us where we could find the lady who'd been Mr. Amberly's nurse.

She barely glanced at me, but gave Felicia a slowly deliberate once-over.

"You look like a movie actress," she said at last.

"Which one?" asked Felicia.

"None in particular. You're just very unusually gorgeous."

"Well, what a charming young lady! Can you help us?"

"Why do you want the nurse?"

"It's rather complicated, dear. Mr. Wilcox is a private investigator I've hired to check into the deaths of my uncle and Mr. Edwards. You know about Mr. Edwards?"

"Oh yes! He was murdered. You think your uncle was murdered too?" It was plain the idea appealed to her.

"Well, it's all very confidential, so please don't mention it to anyone, but we have reasons to be suspicious."

"Just a minute," said the girl, "I'll go check with Grandma."

Minutes later she led us through a large vestibule into a living room not much bigger than a city railroad station. It ran strong on red, deep cushions, thick carpets, and general show-off, and had enough lamps to light Saint Paul. The fireplace was a humble affair you could cook a steer in.

A chair by the hearth big enough to double as a bed held a fat lady stretched out like an overstuffed Cleopatra barging down the Nile. Her examination of us was slower than her granddaughter's, and like hers, found more pleasure in looking at Felicia than me. Glances my way were grudging all through the interview. She sent her granddaughter for a notebook where she had the nurse's address, and was per-

fectly willing to discuss her late neighbor and activities in
his household.

The tall man, she told us, had shown up around the first
of the year. He spent a great deal of time at the house and
more than once took the nurse places in his Packard.

"I suspect they were attracted to each other because they
were both so tall. Of course she didn't measure up to him,
but she was certainly a head taller than any other woman
I've known."

"You think they were intimate?" Felicia asked.

"They were discreet. I never observed any actions or ges-
tures that'd suggest improprieties—except for the fact they
rode often together and she stayed out late several evenings.
I couldn't believe Mr. Amberly would've approved if he'd
been aware—which he probably wasn't. He was anything
but alert in his last few months."

"Would you say he was senile?" I asked.

"No," she said, giving me one of her rare, grudging
glances. "Occasionally absent a little, but senile? No. Do you
really believe there was foul play in his death?"

"It seems a possibility," said Felicia.

"Well, I'm sure he was very vulnerable. It wouldn't have
been hard to do away with him."

We talked a little more but came up with nothing signif-
icant. Felicia thanked her for the address and we left.

The nurse's home was in humbler surroundings, about
six blocks west of Amberly's place. The front door screen
was full of small tears and sagged outward. I told Felicia they
probably had a big cat who climbed it often trying to gain
admission.

A stocky woman in white answered my knock.

I said we were looking for the lady who'd been Mr.
Amberly's nurse. She said wait. Soon a woman, easily my
height, approached the screen from the inside gloom.

"I'm Idella Perkins," she said. Thick hair, mostly brown
but with tinges of red, framed an oval face and a wide, soft
mouth. Her dark eyes took in Felicia's face and mine.

I introduced us. She said, "Oh, Lyman's niece!" and gently pushed the screen open so we could step back and around it. She apologized for the screen's condition. "My mother's tomcat climbs it when we don't let him in at first yowl. In fact now he climbs it before yowling and, if it's unlatched, sways back and forth on it so it slams horribly."

We entered a small light living room to the left of a stairway with a wrought-iron railing and were waved to a couch backed up to the windows. She took an easy chair in a corner beside the entrance to a dining room and asked what she could do for us.

She spoke politely as her brown eyes examined first Felicia and then me with something like kindly tolerance.

"I assume," said Felicia, "that you've heard of Felton Edwards's murder?"

"Of course," she said, looking mournful. "A ghastly thing."

"I understand he visited my uncle often. Did you know what sort of business he had with him?"

"Well, I'm a nurse, not a financial advisor. I didn't pay close attention to their conversations in that line."

"You don't know what kind of investment Edwards offered?" I asked.

"I'm afraid not."

"What sort of condition was Mr. Amberly in during his last six months? Did you think he was senile?"

"No. He was occasionally forgetful, sometimes distracted, but his problems were mostly physical. He was run down and paying the price for a long disregard of proper diet and exercise."

"Then you don't think he could have been easily conned?" I asked.

She smiled condescendingly. "Mr. Amberly was more likely to be the wolf than the sheep, even in his declining months."

"Did you hear any talk about bars Edwards was planning to open?"

"I did not. He never mentioned anything like that in my hearing. I know there've been wild stories about his involvement with illicit liquor during Prohibition, but I doubt he'd have been interested in new enterprises in that line at this late date."

"Did my uncle have someone come in to do cleaning, laundry, and other chores?" asked Felicia.

"Oh yes. A cleaning lady came in three times a week. She took the washing to a friend of hers. I did most of the cooking and dishes, even though they weren't my responsibility. Mr. Amberly slept a good deal and was quite undemanding. There's a limit to how much time I can spend reading, so I didn't mind the chores outside my professional duties. Especially for a man as fine as Mr. Amberly."

Felicia failed to conceal her annoyance with this line and asked if her uncle had ever spoken of her.

"Yes, he did." Idella Perkins gave her a sweet smile. "He said you were a handsome woman who married very cleverly."

It was plain Felicia didn't consider that flattering, and after we got the cleaning lady's address we left promptly.

"She's lying," snarled Felicia as she scrambled into our Dodge.

"About what?"

"Everything. Particularly about Lyman being nice. He was irascible, peevish, demanding, and abusive."

"How'd you know that?"

"I met him. He came east five or six years ago. He was an impossible man then, and I'll not believe he improved with age."

"The lady said he approved of your looks."

"Oh yes, and didn't she just let me know he thought I was a gold digger?"

We drove to the address the lady had given us for the cleaning woman and met a wizened crone with dyed black hair, hunched shoulders, and clawish hands. I guessed the local kids had her pegged as a witch.

"Yes," she said, speaking to us from behind her screen door, "I remember the tall man. Always waving his arms, talking, laying on the sweet like it was maple syrup and we were waffles. I'd ask you in but the place's a mess. Don't have time for my own cleaning, just do it for folks that pay. Why don't we go over to Gottsleben's for a cuppa coffee and chat?"

We drove about six blocks while the witch lady stroked the car upholstery and beamed at pedestrians. She paraded us into the restaurant, demanded and got a corner table, and ordered coffee and four raised doughnuts, which she devoured daintily while swigging from her cup. She watched Felicia as if she were a princess, obviously envying her looks, clothes, and style.

Yes, we learned, the tall man had visited the Amberly place often, two or three times a week at first, then almost daily. He was making a play, she said, for Lyman's money and Idella's body.

"You could see they was right for each other, both so tall and slim. She sure never saw another man'd have her, even though she's not bad-looking. Tall wimmin scare men. I cleaned up the ashtrays he left all the time, and since he wasn't hardly ever around when I was, I knew he come evenings."

She said she'd never heard conversations between the tall man and Mr. Amberly .

"What'd the old man die of?" I asked.

"Just wore out. He was real old—eighty, maybe even ninety. Old, old man. Just lay his head down and died one night."

She picked at the crumbs on her plate and I asked if she'd like another doughnut.

It took a second for her to decide no.

"Too self-indulgent."

We drove her home, said good-bye, and left.

"You think Felton might've murdered my uncle?" Felicia asked.

"Probably not. But I wonder if our Idella might've thought it'd be helpful?"

"To Felton?"

"To her. Maybe she'd already managed to get named in your uncle's will and didn't want Felton taking a slice out before he cashed in."

"Ah yes, but everyone seems to have thought they were pretty involved with each other."

"She didn't strike me as a lady in mourning. It was closer to gloating."

Felicia finally smiled.

"You're smarter than you look. She isn't in mourning at all, she inherited the whole estate. That's why I hired Eric and why I came to see for myself."

26

Felicia's smile vanished the minute she finished her announcement, and I decided she was afraid overdoing it would give her laugh wrinkles.

We drove to the police station from the cleaning lady's place, and Sergeant Wendtland showed more warmth than I'd ever seen when I approached his desk alone. His grin about dimpled his ears and I guessed it was caused by my partner's looks and not his anticipation of me catching hell from his boss, which had been the case in most of my past visits. That was reinforced when he got up and escorted us to Baker's office.

Baker's reaction as I introduced Felicia about made me think I needed a new introduction myself. He rose from his desk, hustled around to greet us, shook hands, and was warm and sweet-natured as a preacher hosting the ladies' aid. Once we were all seated he immediately began telling me how I should get at finding Felton's killer.

"The only logical perpetrator," he explained grandly, "has to be Les Clint, the cuckolded man in the case. Get back to his daughter—she's the one he cares about and he'll be in touch with her. Count on it."

He beamed at Felicia. "When you've had as much experience as I have, you know these things, no matter how complicated they look at first, are simple in the end. This Clint guy's not the kind to change his name and start a new life in South America. He's a born citizen, you know? All routine, responsibility, and habit. When his kind busts loose and kills, the minute it's over he's back to old Joe Citizen again. He can no more handle being a fugitive than he could fly. You got to understand the psychology of people to deal with crimes of passion."

He turned to me again, like old dad.

"Find Les Clint and the whole thing solves itself."

It was enough to make my tired ache.

Felicia's sober face made him decide maybe he was talking too much, and he switched tactics and asked how she happened to be in this territory.

She allowed herself a one-second smile and told him she was in South Dakota for two reasons; one, as a professional writer, the other, as the niece of Mr. Amberly, an Aquatown citizen who'd died recently. As a writer she was interested in the area in general and was doing an article on its people and economics. She'd become interested in the murder of Felton Edwards because it was such a traumatic event in a peaceful community, but also because the man had spent much of his last days alive in conferences with her uncle, whose death barely preceded his.

Baker took it all in, nodding. Finally he pulled his mitts off the desk, tilted his chair back, and clasped his fingers behind his bullet head.

"You figure he might've been pulling a con on your uncle?"

"Well," said Felicia, "I doubt he came around just to enrich the last days of a dying old man. The most interesting thing, however, is that the nurse, whom Mr. Edwards was giving a big rush, is the sole beneficiary of my uncle's will."

Baker's cold-fish eyes blinked. He tilted his chair forward and put his elbows on the desk.

"You planning to contest it?"

"If I can get information that'll make it seem practical, yes."

"How?"

Felicia allowed another smile and said, "I think there should be an autopsy on Uncle Lyman's body."

Baker was brought up short and stared at her a moment through his thick-lensed glasses. His magnified eyes reminded me that he was about as warmblooded as a rattlesnake.

"What's your uncle got to do with Felton's death?"

"I don't know that it has anything to do with it. It just happens I think he was murdered, and want to get to the bottom of it."

"An autopsy's not easy to get once a man's been planted. You got any solid evidence to back up your notions?"

"There's a check missing from Uncle Lyman's bankbook. I've no evidence it's been cashed, but it's odd, because he was fanatically fussy about money."

"You talk with the doc who certified the death?"

"I talked with him on the telephone. He was vague and condescending at first. When I pressed him he became defensive and tried to intimidate me with medical jargon. When I explained the reasons for my suspicions he became rude."

"Yeah, sounds like Doc Goeschy. Turns porcupine the minute anybody doesn't swallow his guff like gospel. Okay, I'll put the proposition to Judge Long. He's been sore at Goeschy a couple times, might get a kick out of embarrassing him."

Felicia produced a two-hundred-watt smile that dazzled him so thoroughly he promised to make arrangements first thing in the morning.

Back in the car Felicia decided she needed to buy some things in town, and we agreed to meet at five and take off for Hope. As soon as I dropped her at the department store I drove back to Idella Perkins's house. She answered the door herself, showed no surprise at seeing me, and agreed to talk. Without Felicia's presence, Idella was relaxed and even friendly.

I explained I wanted to know when she'd seen Felton last and if he'd mentioned anything about where he was going next.

"It was the Sunday before his death. He asked me to marry him."

She watched me closely as she said that, and smiled.

"What'd you say?"

"No."

"Why?"

"I knew he was an opportunist. He'd been trying to get Mr. Amberly's money; failing in that, he hoped to get it through me."

"He knew Amberly was leaving his wad to you?"

"Oh yes. I told him. He was amusing for a time, but actually, the only thing we had in common was being too tall. I guess you don't know what that's like."

"It's never ben a problem for me," I admitted. "Mrs. Amberly's attorney thought you were defensive when you talked with him."

"That lawyer was looking for ways to challenge the will. I wasn't about to help him."

"How'd Felton handle your turn-down?"

"Rather well, actually. At first he got mad, but finally he laughed and said I was smart. He tried to convince me we could do very well together. I made it clear I'd done fine on my own and didn't need him. We shook hands and he left. I've no idea what plans he had, but I'm certain he was busy making them from the moment I rejected him. He didn't say where he was going next, and I didn't ask."

"Did you know there was a check missing from Amberly's book?"

I thought she looked surprised, but then she shook her head. "No, I never looked at his private papers. Where'd you hear that?"

"His niece, Felicia. Who was the will's executor?"

"Wesley Tucker, his attorney."

She walked me to the door and, when I stopped to thank her for her time, smiled and asked, "Have you ever wished you were tall?"

"Yeah, right now."

Her laugh followed me down the walk.

▽

27

Before meeting Felicia I tried calling old Amberly's attorney, but his secretary told me he was out for the rest of the day and she didn't know where he could be reached.

About five miles out of Aquatown I glanced at Felicia and said I'd had a little conference with her uncle's attorney. Her head jerked and her body went stiff as she turned to stare at me.

"Who?"

"Wes Tucker. The executor of your uncle's will."

Her mouth was tight as she looked at the dusty graveled road ahead. "Why'd you call him?"

"Wanted to see if he knew about the missing check."

Her expression made me think she'd start screaming at me, but in a second she controlled it and shook her head.

"You shouldn't have done that. It could ruin everything."

"You maybe lied a little to Baker, right?"

"I had to give him something to work with. It could be true, for all I know. Now the attorney will be talking to the police and they won't do the autopsy."

"Well, don't fret, Felicia. I lied a little too. The lawyer wasn't in when I called."

Her body went loose and she slumped against the car door

a second. Then she straightened up and moved a couple inches my way.

"You're very devious and tricky," she said. "I'm really surprised at you."

"But you like that in a man, right?"

She turned on the seat, pulled her left leg up so her knee was just touching my thigh, and propped her left arm on the seat back.

"What I think," she said, "is that pair of giraffes killed my uncle after spending six months working on him to get his will changed, and when it was done, that woman killed Felton so he couldn't blackmail her and dumped him in the sandpit."

"Why'd she pick a sandpit in Hope?"

"She probably heard about it from him. How do I know? But the murder makes sense for her."

I granted that.

She straightened around and stared through the windshield as a car approached, laying its rolling yellow dust cloud. I wound up my side window until the car was past and the cloud had been swept away by the prairie wind.

"God, what a miserable country," she said. "No wonder people go crazy and kill each other . . ."

I dropped her off at the hotel in Hope, returned the car to Severance's garage, and went over to see Ruppman. He listened to my selective report of the trip, conceding that it had been a little better than the last, since now we knew part of what the hell Felton had been up to since leaving Edenberg. He said there'd been no further word on Les Clint. His wife claimed she'd heard nothing, the daughter likewise. The son, when Ruppman reached him by phone in Missouri, said he hadn't seen or heard from his old man in months, and made it clear he liked it that way.

I went back to the hotel, took a shower, got into fresh duds, and telephoned Mac McGillacuddy's aunt. I asked if she'd be willing to cook up steaks if I brought some around. She said it'd beat the hash she'd been planning to cook.

The butcher fixed me up with three T-bones, and a little after six that evening Florence, Mac, and I were hard at work on them with fried onions, hash brown potatoes, and green peas. Afterward there was green-apple pie, vanilla ice cream, and finally coffee.

I was hoping Mac would go to bed early, or maybe I could take Florence for a long walk to a peaceful thicket, but he stuck around after dishes and we gabbed. I asked if he'd swung around the sandpit lately and he said not since the day before yesterday.

"Tired of it?" I asked. "No new bodies?"

"It smells bad," he said.

"Yeah? Like what?"

"Just bad."

"Like an outhouse?"

"No. Worse."

Florence thought we should talk about something more pleasant at the table, but I asked where he'd noticed the smell and he said near where we'd found Felton.

Florence told Mac it was time he thought about getting ready for bed. He looked resigned and went upstairs.

"I suppose you've got a spade for the garden?" I asked Florence.

"Yes, of course. Why?"

"I'd like to borrow it."

She stared at me for a moment. "Mac gave you an idea, didn't he?"

"Yeah."

"You think somebody was buried there, in the sandpit. Is that it?"

"Uh-huh. Guy named Leslie Clint, I'd guess. If you don't mind, I'll check it out."

She sighed. "The spade's in the basement. I'll get it."

▽

28

THERE WAS NO MOON so the stars had the sky all to themselves and the Milky Way gave light enough to make shadows.

Florence loaned me a flashlight along with the spade and I left her house by the back door and hiked cross-country northwest toward the sandpit. It occurred to me Ruppman might be watching the place but I saw no sign of him and felt fairly sure he didn't have the back covered. Just in case, I stopped often to look around the pastureland that sloped up toward the west and east to the backside of the business area and homes along the main drag, where streetlights were shaded by trees and the water tower glowed feebly against the dark northeastern sky. A truck rumbled along the country road behind me, a dog barked off to the south, and a million crickets made their racket in steady rhythm across the prairie.

The sandpit, when I approached, looked wide and deep as the Grand Canyon, stretched out there in the dark.

I stopped at its southeast edge, where the road made its entry, and stared into the blackness. It seemed solid enough to reflect the sky like a calm lake. Instead, it just swallowed all the light. I shifted the spade from my right to my left hand, took the flashlight from under my belt, and turned it on. My world narrowed down to the spot of light at the end of the broadening beam.

Near the floor of the pit the sound of crickets became faint. I turned off the flash and looked up at the stars. They'd moved closer, like a lowered lid. After a moment I could see the truck ruts, and even make out low and high spots around me.

It seemed a long walk to where Felton Edwards's body had lain, and the stink reached me long before I could center the right spot. It was halfway between the sand slope's edge and the rut road along the northwest end. I circled it three times, breathing through my mouth and moving out farther about a yard at a time, and finally located a softer area. The flashlight showed signs that something had been digging, but had not gone far. I kicked up a small mound of sand, placed the flashlight on its top pointing toward my target, and started digging. I'd not moved more than a dozen spadefuls when I heard a sound from the ridge on the south.

I jumped for the light, snapped it off, dashed to the nearest mound, scrambled over, swung around, and flattened out. A car without lights eased over the pit edge and came along the road toward me, so slow and careful the motor was hardly loud enough to cover the sound of its tires rolling on sand as the car pulled off the ruts. The big motor purred softly a few moments before the driver shut it off and I could hear distant crickets again and pings from the cooling engine.

The driver's door opened, the dome light came on, and a man emerged, his head deep in shadows. Mrs. Pauline Clint sat in the passenger's seat, her face white, her eyes dark with makeup. The man straightened and closed the door behind him carefully and the light snapped off. I caught a glimpse of his face as he looked around. Then he moved to where I'd dug, turned a flashlight on, and ran the beam over the sandy ground until it stopped at the opening I'd begun. The light jerked. He moved closer, stood erect, and shot the beam all around. I ducked my head, smacking my forehead into the sand so hard I thought he'd hear the impact.

His feet crunched in movement. I lifted my head, opened my eyes, saw no light, and raised myself enough to see the man standing beside the car window.

The voice was too low to hear. I pulled together, got into a low crouch, and moved in a half circle toward the back of the car, which, I suddenly realized, was a hearse.

The guy straightened again and started toward the back. I froze. He opened the rear door, pulled out a shovel, and headed for the pit grave.

I edged toward the car, sat, and watched him work. He wasn't real good at it, but whoever'd done the burying hadn't gotten carried away, so it didn't take long before he was hauling at the body, trying to pull it clear of the sand. The sides where he'd dug gave way, and he slipped, went to his knees, and swore.

"Come here," he called, trying to keep it low but it came out harsh in the night.

The dome light flared as Mrs. Clint opened the door, got out, and moved toward him. I saw a purse in her hand and wondered why she thought she'd need it now.

"He's heavy," complained the man. "I'll need help. Take the feet."

"I can't," she said flatly. "The smell's making me sick."

"Jesus Christ, breathe through your mouth. I can't do this alone!"

"Don't panic," she said in a tone that'd frost live coals, "drag him."

He swore and said all right then, move the goddamn car closer to the body.

She went back, started the engine, and turned on the lights. He screamed at her to turn them off, which she did at once. By then she was rattled. She made the car jump when she got it in gear, and sent sand flying from the rear wheels. I scuttled back a ways and watched as she maneuvered the big car awkwardly around and slowly backed it toward the waiting man. She stopped too soon and he told her to move another yard. She went almost two and damned near ran over him.

When he grasped the corpse under the armpits and started heaving it into the rear of the hearse I moved, and was at his side by the time he had it almost in. Pauline screamed at the sight of me.

He jerked around and I swung the flat of the spade into his belly hard enough to lift his feet and lay him flat. Pauline popped out of the car, fumbling at her purse, and jerked back, making me miss a jab at her with the spade handle. I jabbed again, caught her right shoulder, and deflected the shot she snapped off before I closed on her wrist.

She bit, clawed, kicked, and screamed until I got her turned over, worked an arm lock on the gun side, and applied a chokehold on her neck. When she went limp I let go and turned her head so she wouldn't breathe sand, even though a part of me wanted to just shove her head into it. That was the part that'd been scratched, bitten, and kicked.

I found her gun where she'd dropped it, went over to McCoy, and got him sitting up. He kept groaning and saying I'd broken his innards.

"Just be glad I didn't swing lower, Big Dick," I said. "At least your main attraction's still intact."

Eventually I got him up and he managed to help his lady love into the front seat of the hearse. I sat in back with the gun at his head while he drove into town, following my directions to City Hall.

29

Naturally, when I got to City Hall Ruppman wasn't around, and I assumed he was out policing lover's lanes or protecting nearby watermelon patches and crab apple trees. I locked Pauline in the single cell and took McCoy back to Ruppman's crummy office.

He slumped forlornly on the wooden chair. I took the swivel job, put the gun on the desk beside me, and gave the prisoner my best sympathetic smile.

"Let's get it out of your system," I said. "What happened, did the husband who was supposed to be on his way to Minneapolis show up when you were making out with his wife, and one of you shot him, just to calm him down?"

"It wasn't like that at all. I wasn't even in the house when he died."

"So tell me about it."

"What's the use? You aren't gonna believe it."

"Probably not, but what the hell've you got to lose? Give me a try."

"What happened was, that goddamned Felton heard Les was gonna be out of town and he came around to try and make Polly. She was fighting him off when old Les suddenly showed up with his gun, crazy mad. He told them right off he didn't give a damn about them screwing each other but he was going to shoot Felton because he'd tried to screw his little girl, Elaine, when she was only fourteen. Polly screamed that he was a liar and flew at him, they fought for the gun, and it went off and killed Les deader than an old mackerel. Then Polly and Felton got into it and he told her if she didn't go along with him she'd be the one to go to prison for the killing, so she broke down and agreed to help and they put Les in the hearse and drove him to the sandpit there in Hope and buried him. But while she was watching Felton work the shovel Polly got more and more upset about it all. She took the gun he'd left in the hearse, and when he was through burying Les, she shot Felton. Then she went through his pockets to be sure he didn't have anything on him that'd connect with Les—"

"Like what?"

"Well, earlier that day, before Les knew this thing about Felton trying to do Elaine, Les agreed to give Felton money for his idea of setting up a bar. I guess he figured it like a payoff—he'd give Felton the money and Felton'd leave Polly alone. So he gave Felton a check. So while she was at it, Polly took Felton's wallet and everything else, figuring maybe the cops'd decide it was simple robbery. Polly doesn't think much of cops and she told me they'd be real happy to settle for the simplest solution. Old Ruppman would've, from what I hear."

"So how'd you wind up helping Polly dig up the corpse for a transfer?"

"Well, the fact is, it's all your fault. When you first showed up asking questions she figured you were just a moron hick without a chance of figuring any of it out, but when you kept digging around and even talked to her daughter in Minneapolis and all that, she got scared and told me one night what'd really happened and begged me to help her. She started thinking Felton hadn't buried Les deep enough and a dog'd dig him up or something like that. I don't know what happened yesterday that got her over the edge, but she called

me at work and said she had to see me and we met and she
said Les's body had to be moved that night and if I didn't
help her she'd be convicted of murdering her husband and
Felton, and only I could save her. What could I do, spit in
her eye? I really love her, you know? She's more than any
other woman I've ever met and none of all this was really her
fault, it was because Felton was a son of a bitch and it was
all his doing."

"I can see that," I said, not lying too much. "The only
thing that still bothers me is why you killed Maxie. Why was
he a threat?"

"I didn't kill him. He died of smoke from a fire he caused
himself. He didn't have anything to do with anything but
trying to get the body hidden where nobody'd find it."

"Don't kid me. Maxie and Felton were real buddies. Got
together and talked regular. The way I figure it, Felton told
Maxie he was going to get a check from Les the day before
Les was leaving for Minneapolis, and I'd guess, Felton being
like he was, told old Maxie he planned not only to take Les's
money, but screw his wife the same night. I think that would
have given those two guys a big laugh. And when Felton
turned up dead, and Les missing, I think Maxie gave the
missus a call and suggested maybe she owed him a little
something for keeping his mouth shut. And then Polly re-
cruited you to do a little smoke job. You did it so fine it nearly
worked. Maxie was probably waiting for you to come and
make the payoff. You had a couple drinks with him and
slipped him something and, when he turned peaceful,
dropped his lighted cigarette on the mattress, gave it a few
puffs to encourage it, and quietly went back to screw Polly."

"You can't prove that," he said.

"It won't be easy—but that's what happened, isn't it?"

"I'm not gonna talk to you anymore. I don't have to. You
aren't even the real cop here."

"That's right. But it'll all come out."

"No it won't. You got it all too complicated and Polly's
right, cops like it simple. So do juries. You can't prove a

damned thing and I'll deny everything I've told you."

"That's what I figured. But you see, killers aren't the only ones that can lie. Think how simple it'll get for Ruppman if I tell him what you said and he decides he was here with me when you confessed. That'll make everything pretty simple, won't it?"

For a second I thought he was going to try for the gun but I put my hand on it, not wanting to bang him around any more. He settled back, pretending unconcern, but I could see the defeat in his eyes.

"The real clincher," I said, "is your lady love'll make the whole business your fault. She'll claim you shot both Les and Felton, and did Maxie on top of it. Face it, McCoy, you're bound to be the fall guy. Your only chance is to level and get off easier. You clam up and it'll all be on you. Polly's lots better-looking to any jury you're likely to see in South Dakota."

"You don't know Polly," he said.

"I know her type," I told him. "She's like you, all for Number One. It comes down to the wire, she sure's hell isn't going to take credit for killing anybody if there's a patsy handy, and McCoy, old buddy, you're just that."

I took him back to the cell, unlocked it, and ordered Pauline out. Then I shoved McCoy in and led the lady back to Ruppman's office. It surprised me that neither of them tried to say anything to the other. I guessed McCoy was trying to figure if I was right about what she'd do and decided to keep shut. She stared at him, figuring it was useless to ask questions then.

Once in the office she took the chair I waved her to and settled into it with her knees and ankles tight together.

"Where's my purse?"

It wasn't a question, it was an accusation.

"I suppose it's in the sandpit where you dropped it when you dug out the gun. Which is in my pocket. What do you want from the purse—your powderpuff, your comb, or the check Felton got from your hubby?"

I thought that speared her but she only blinked and said, "I wanted a cigarette."

"I can roll you one."

"No thank you, I wouldn't care for any of your spit."

"I'd let you lick the paper yourself."

She took a deep breath and leaned against the chair back.

She was figuring out what McCoy had told me, and my crack about the check worried her. If he'd told me that, she no doubt figured he'd unloaded everything.

I gave her my innocent earnest look. "As your boyfriend told me, and you probably know, you don't have to tell me anything. I'm not the local cop, got no authority. But I've been paid to try and work this thing out and right now there's no question about what happened, there's just who's gonna take the rap. It's got to be you or McCoy. One of you's going to spill the beans and get credit for helping the case against the other. That's how it works, you know that, don't you?"

"What'd he tell you?"

I gave her the story, leaving out Maxie.

She listened gravely, after a while lifted her hands and touched her hair absent-mindedly, then trailed them down past her jaw and throat and placed them flat on her smooth thighs.

"Did Elaine really tell you Felton tried to seduce her?"

"Yes."

She tilted her head up and closed her eyes.

"My God, what a sordid mess."

She looked at me.

"Mr. McCoy told you the truth. Les died in the fight for the gun. I'm sure he didn't care. And I killed Felton. I'd do it again. He was the most despicable man I've ever met, I can't believe I let him . . . Well, it's no matter now, is it? I suppose, if you hadn't shown up tonight, I'd have eventually killed Dick McCoy. He wasn't any better than Felton when you come down to it. None of you are worth a damn. Not one."

"Including Maxie, right? Did he try to blackmail you?"

"Of course. Did Dick tell you I was the arsonist?"

I was tempted to say yes, but shook my head. "He wouldn't talk about that. Says Maxie had nothing to do with you."

"He's right. He had nothing to do with any of this, so why make a fuss over that? Two murders should be enough to satisfy any prosecutor."

I agreed, and dropped it.

Ruppman's arrival at least put a stop to our interview, but of course led to more questioning and a lot of carrying on. Finally he telephoned the mayor, waking him from a deep, innocent sleep, and there was talk of where the prisoners should be put, since obviously they couldn't both park in the single cell where they could work on their stories and maybe do something sexually illegal before dawn.

The mayor finally authorized putting Pauline up at the hotel with a deputy on duty in the hall, and Ruppman convinced him that the following day the best move would be to deputize me and send Pauline to Edenberg, where they had a cell fit for a woman. I could at the same time deliver the corpse of Leslie Clint to the coroner there. They actually persuaded Pauline to drive her husband's hearse and body on the trip with me as her passenger guard.

I didn't like any part of it. I refused to carry a gun, thinking that'd squelch the deal, but the mayor said it'd be fine and let me know a little less than subtly how much my cooperation would mean if I ever needed a reference for a future job.

Like they say, you can't fight city hall. I agreed and sacked out.

30

P AULINE TALKED.

She told me her marriage hadn't been successful from the beginning. Les always treated her with all the respect he gave his average corpse and what she wanted was romance, excitement, and a good movie now and then. He didn't like movies, or at least not the ones she did. They didn't fight, she told me, because he had no passion or real spirit. She admitted she'd never been much of a mother. The muss, fuss, and bother drove her crazy and the kids were generally impossible, particularly since Les never took any responsibility for discipline or training. All he wanted was good-night kisses and happy faces.

"He didn't think Elaine could do any wrong or that Sonny could do anything right."

"Sonny's your boy's name?"

"Actually it is. We just somehow started calling him Sonny when he was a baby and it stuck."

That seemed reason enough to alienate a kid from his parents, but I didn't say so.

She was silent for a mile or two and finally gave a sad sigh, throwing me a plaintive look.

"I know I was a fool to underestimate you when we first

met. I like to think I can judge people quick, and usually I've been right. Obviously I was stupid about Les and should've learned from that but—well—anyway, I want to ask you for an opinion because you've had experience with murders, and maybe know some answers I need. Can I talk to you about my defense in this mess?"

"Why not?"

"I couldn't sleep last night, as you might imagine, and mostly I thought about how Elaine and Sonny are going to feel about all this and what could I do to make it a little less horrible. I honestly did not kill Les. It was an accident. Felton got to him when I grabbed Les's wrist and he did the twisting and maybe even managed to squeeze the trigger—I won't harp on it—but it wasn't deliberate murder, it was just a wild scramble and an unlikely shot. The killing of Felton was a reaction to all the horror. I was out of my mind. But it was deliberate too and I'm going to admit that and won't pretend I was temporarily insane. If I say I killed him because he killed Les, do you think my children might believe it and forgive me?"

"It's possible, sure."

"And maybe the prosecution will settle for a single charge of murder and there won't have to be any digging into what happened to that Hicks man and maybe they'll even be willing to say Felton killed Les in self-defense. It was Les's gun, you know—"

"You get a good lawyer, that probably can be worked out, yeah."

"That's what I think. If he's really smart, my lawyer might be able to convince a jury that killing Felton was justifiable homicide."

Her spirits were rising and I didn't try to spike her dream. Hell, maybe she'd actually swing it. The story she was giving me was her test rehearsal and she figured it wasn't bad.

"How about Lois Simpson?" I asked. "McCoy tried to make me think Felton had a thing going with her and that was one of the reasons they stopped being friends. Was there anything to that?"

She laughed. "Of course not. He was just trying to make you think she was the problem so you wouldn't guess about me. He told me all about how clever he'd been. I thought it was stupid. Who'd believe anybody'd get excited about that frump?"

I let her think she had it figured right, but I wasn't really convinced. McCoy, I suspected, had fooled her more than he had me.

In Edenberg, when I turned her over to the head man, she concentrated her charms on him and didn't glance my way as I moved out. I didn't blame her. There was nothing she could hope for from me and she was shrewd enough to concentrate all the powers of her mind and body on survival. It did wonders for her looks. Nobody would guess she hadn't slept the sleep of the true believer.

As I headed back to Hope I thought, God help the prosecutor.

During the next week I painted signs till there were no more and visited Florence each night. The last night I spent in town we almost did it but she stopped me at the edge and said if I gave her some time and came back serious it'd be different.

So I went to Edenberg and called on Agatha, who welcomed me like a hero, smooched with enthusiasm, and in the end turned out no more cooperative than Florence. In her case it annoyed me, and after a week I realized I was too old for high school smooching and gave her up. If that broke her heart she hid it well.

A month later I hit Hope again.

Florence's house was locked up. When I checked with Ruppman at City Hall he informed me with bitter pleasure that in my absence the old flame, Johnnie Powers, had come back. His wife had left him; he got divorced, returned to Hope, and within a week had won Florence back. The house was for sale and she planned to marry the son of a bitch and was househunting in Minneapolis.

For the record, the autopsy on old Amberly only showed

he died of natural causes. Felicia went back east, and I never heard if she sold her story on the quaint folks in South Dakota. I guess Idella lived tall and happy ever after.

Ruppman admitted he'd taken the potshots at me to scare me off, and denied he could've come close enough to make me feel the slug pass by.

The last I heard he was hustling Mary, the waitress at Winkle's.